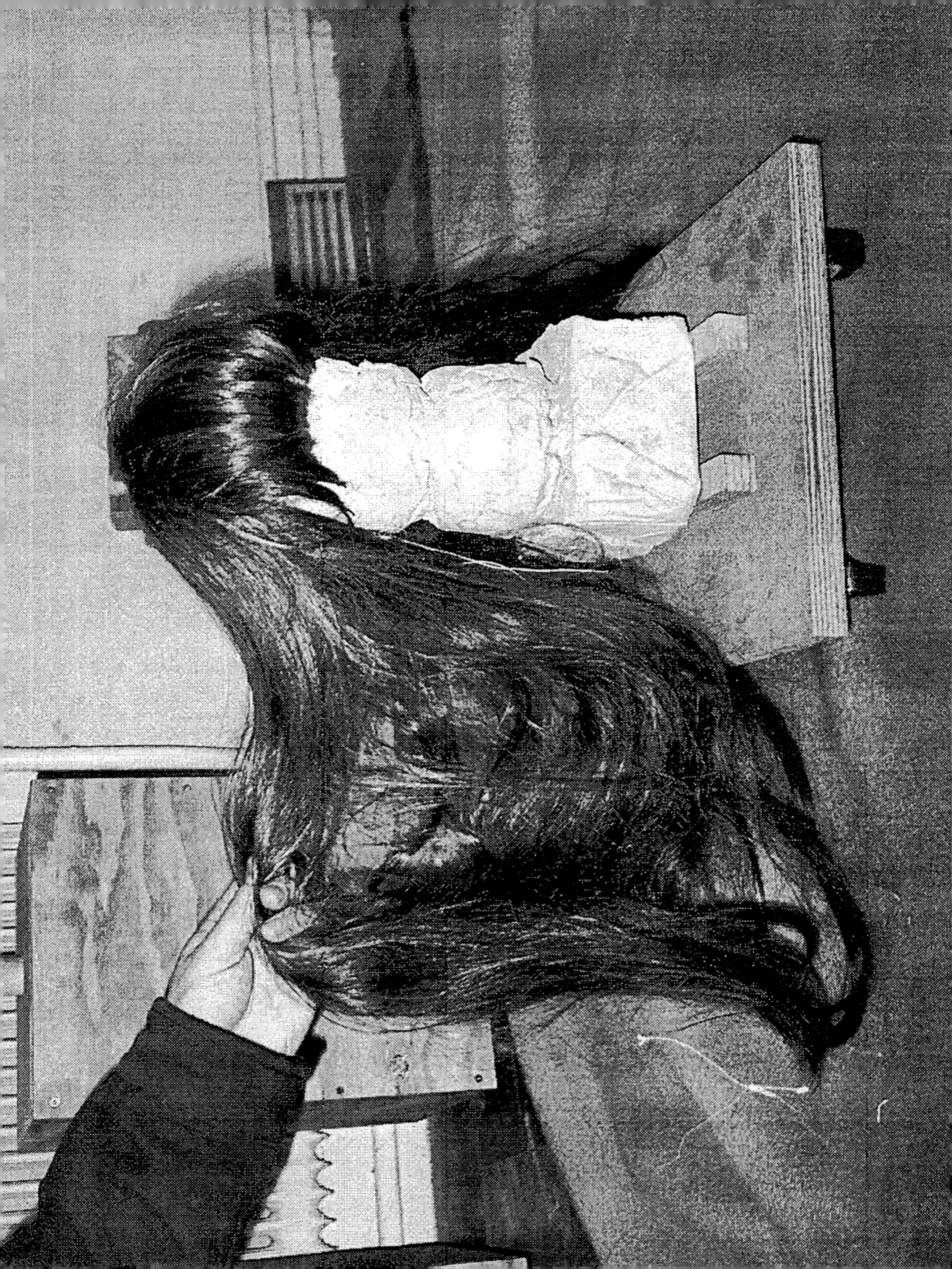

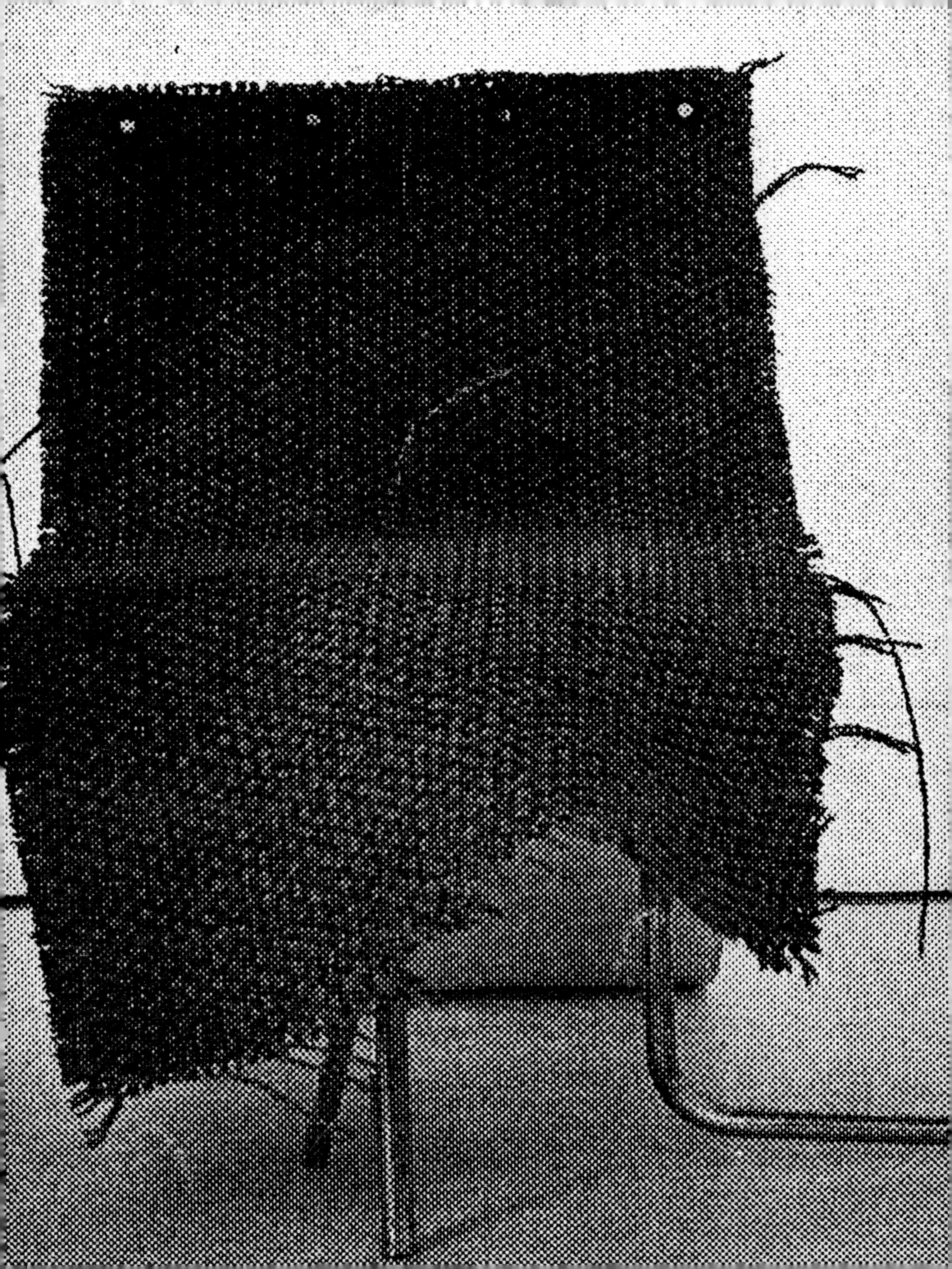

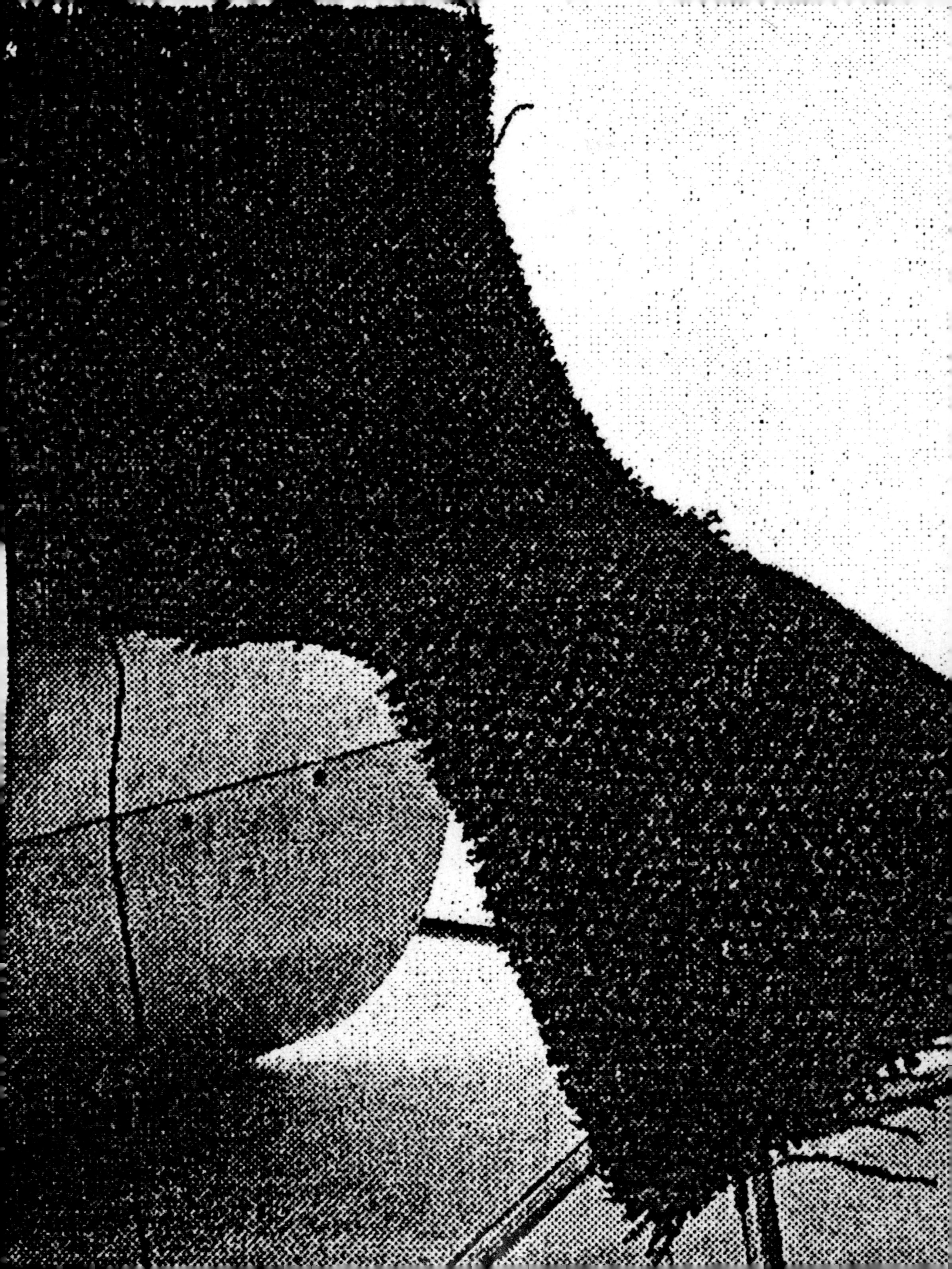

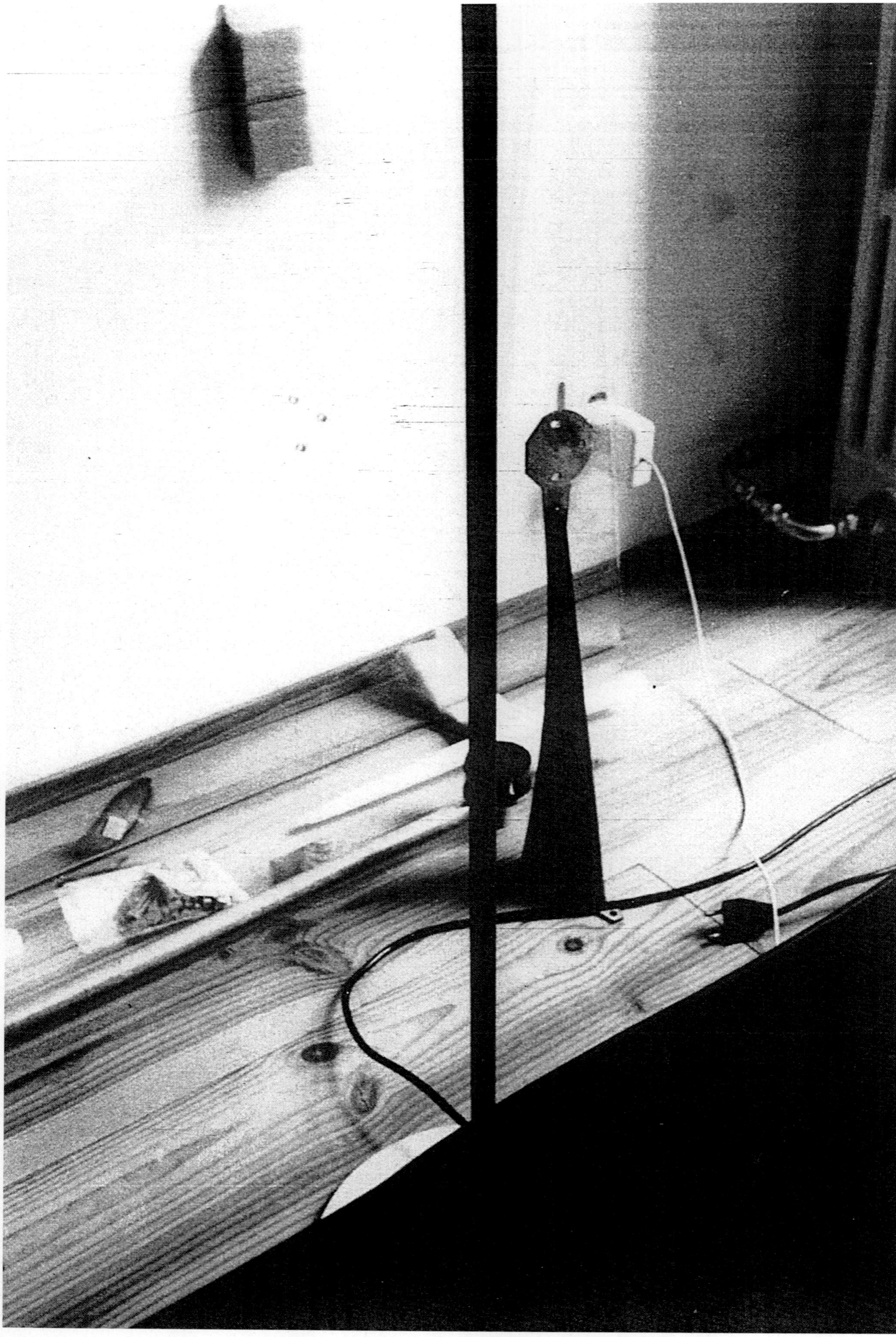

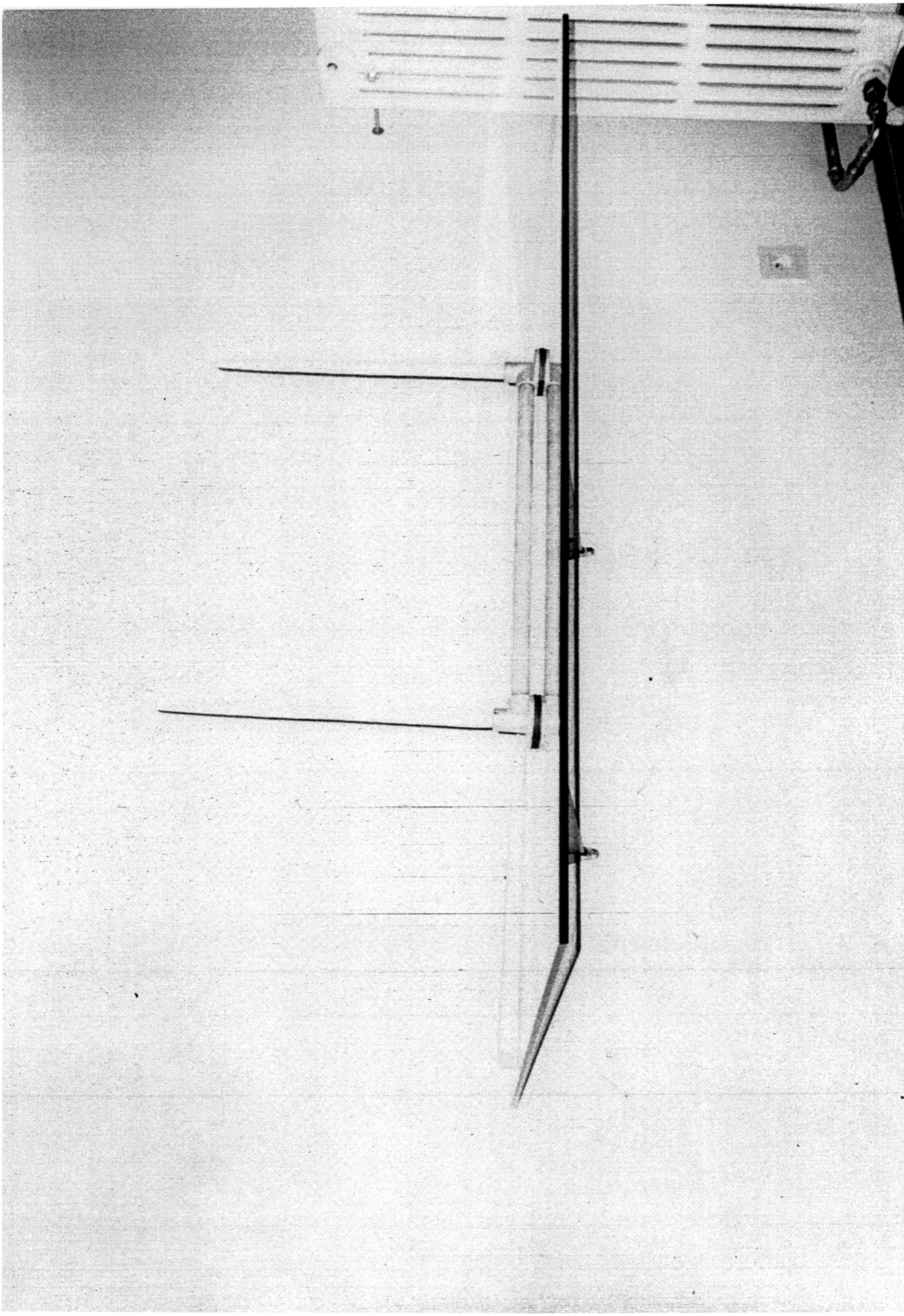

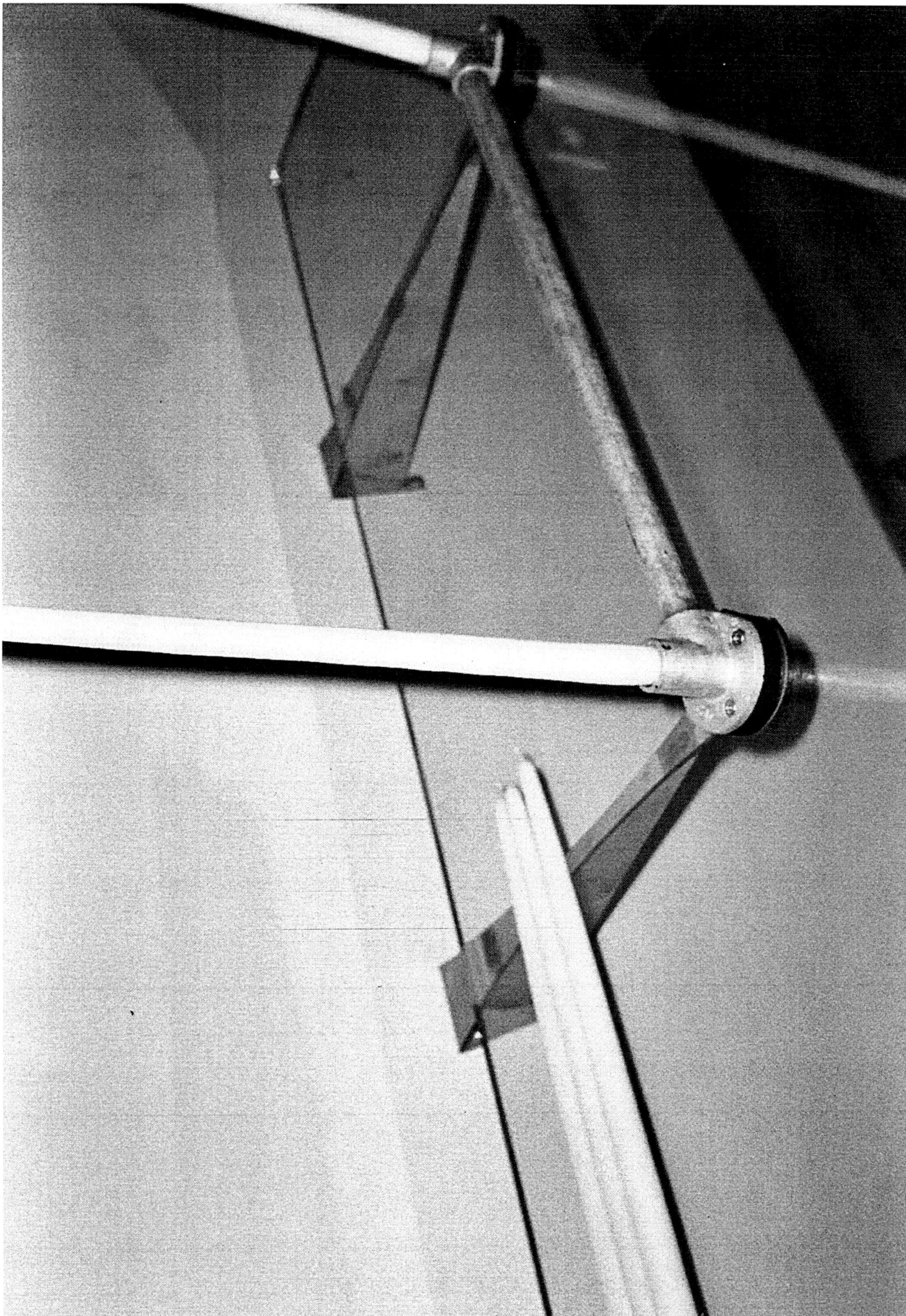

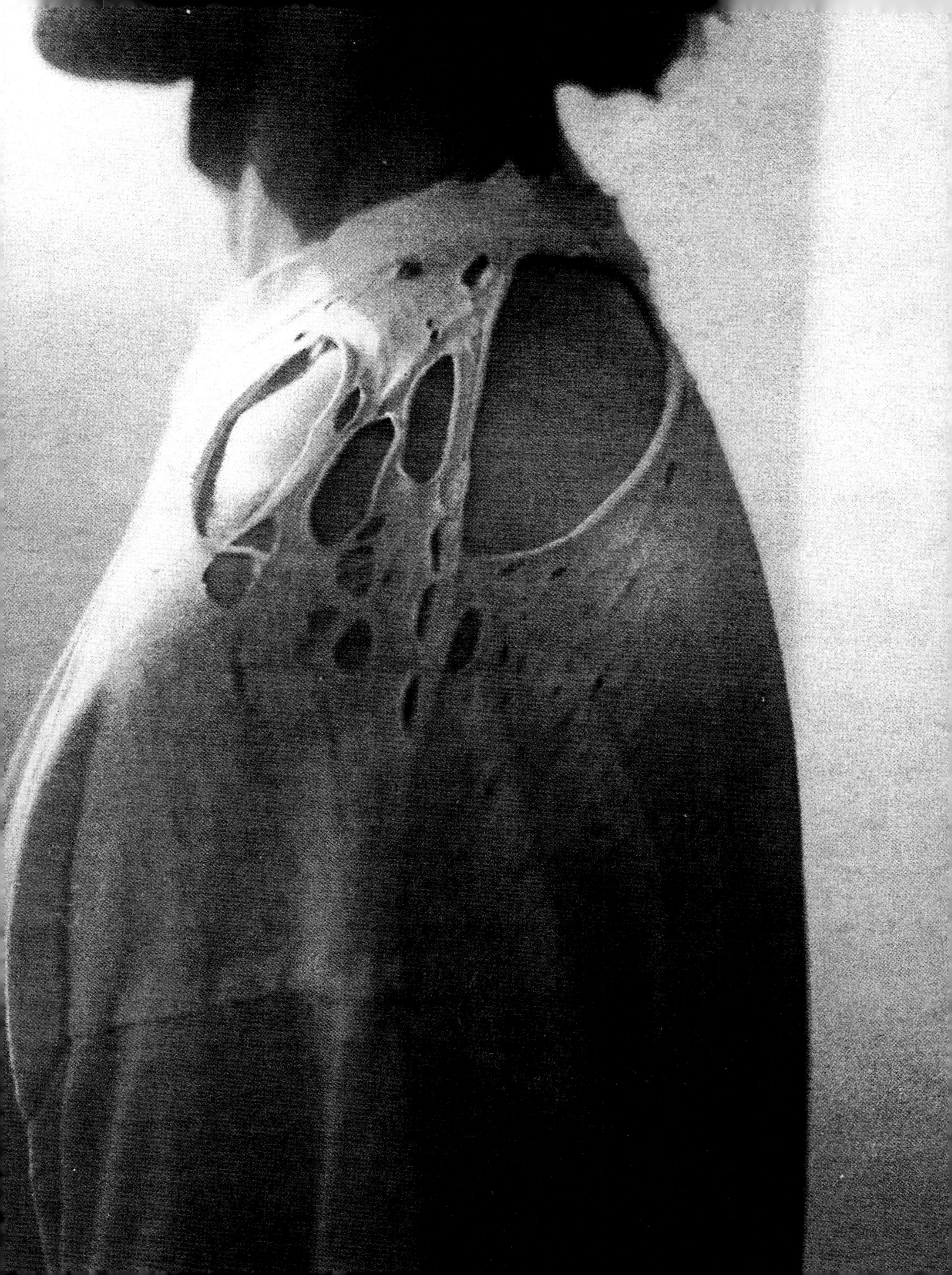

BAYER

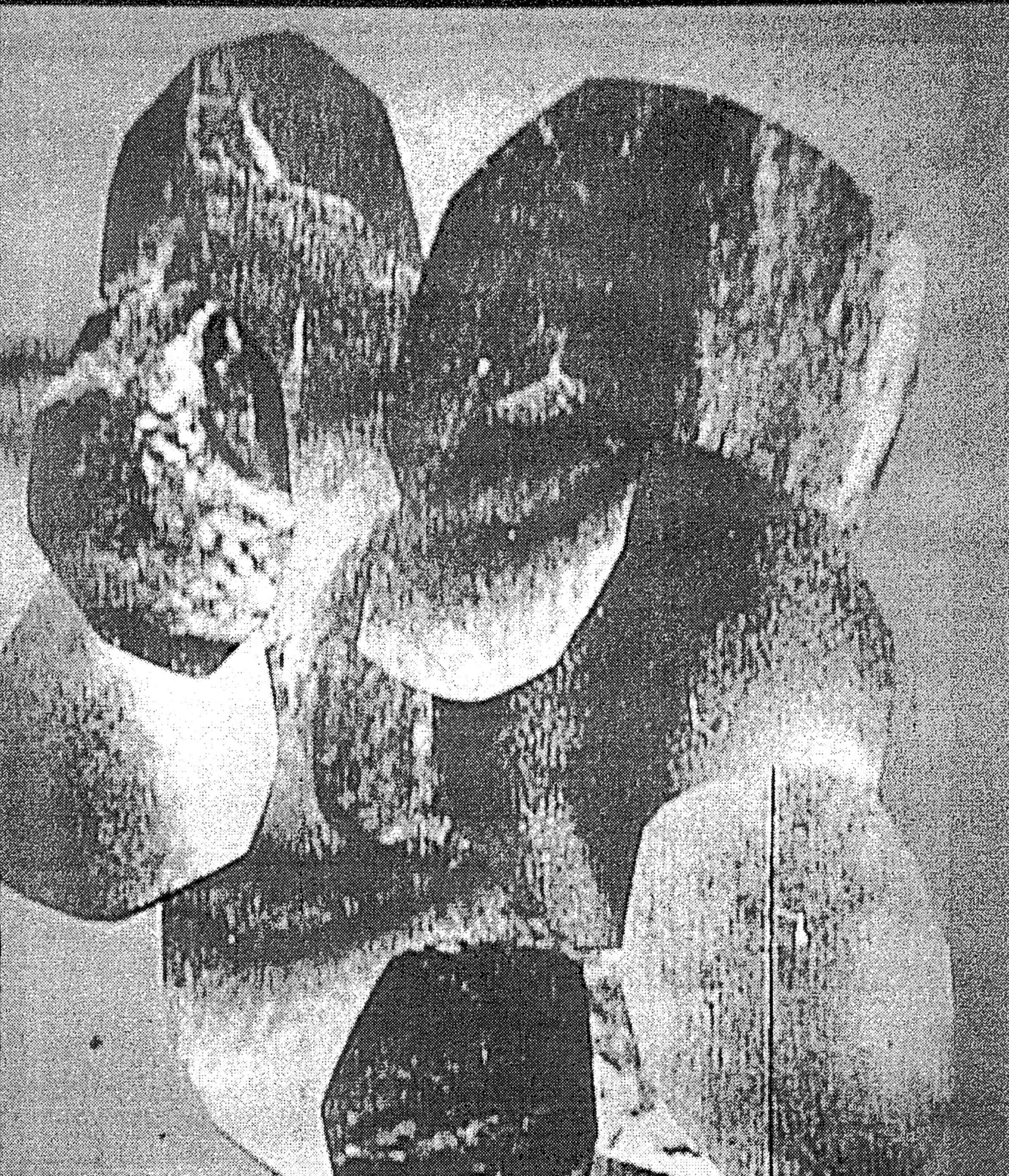

LAOCOON

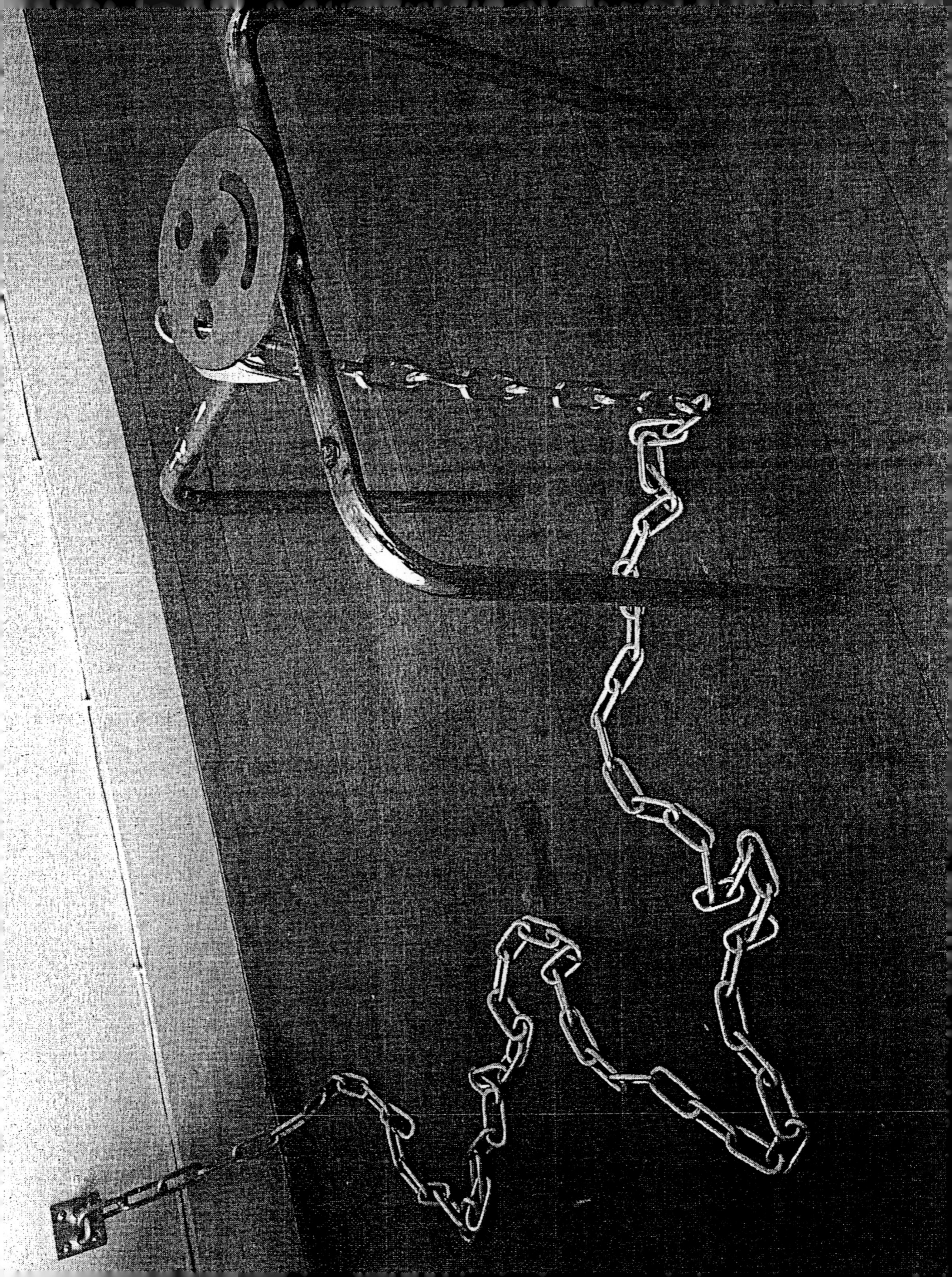

20099

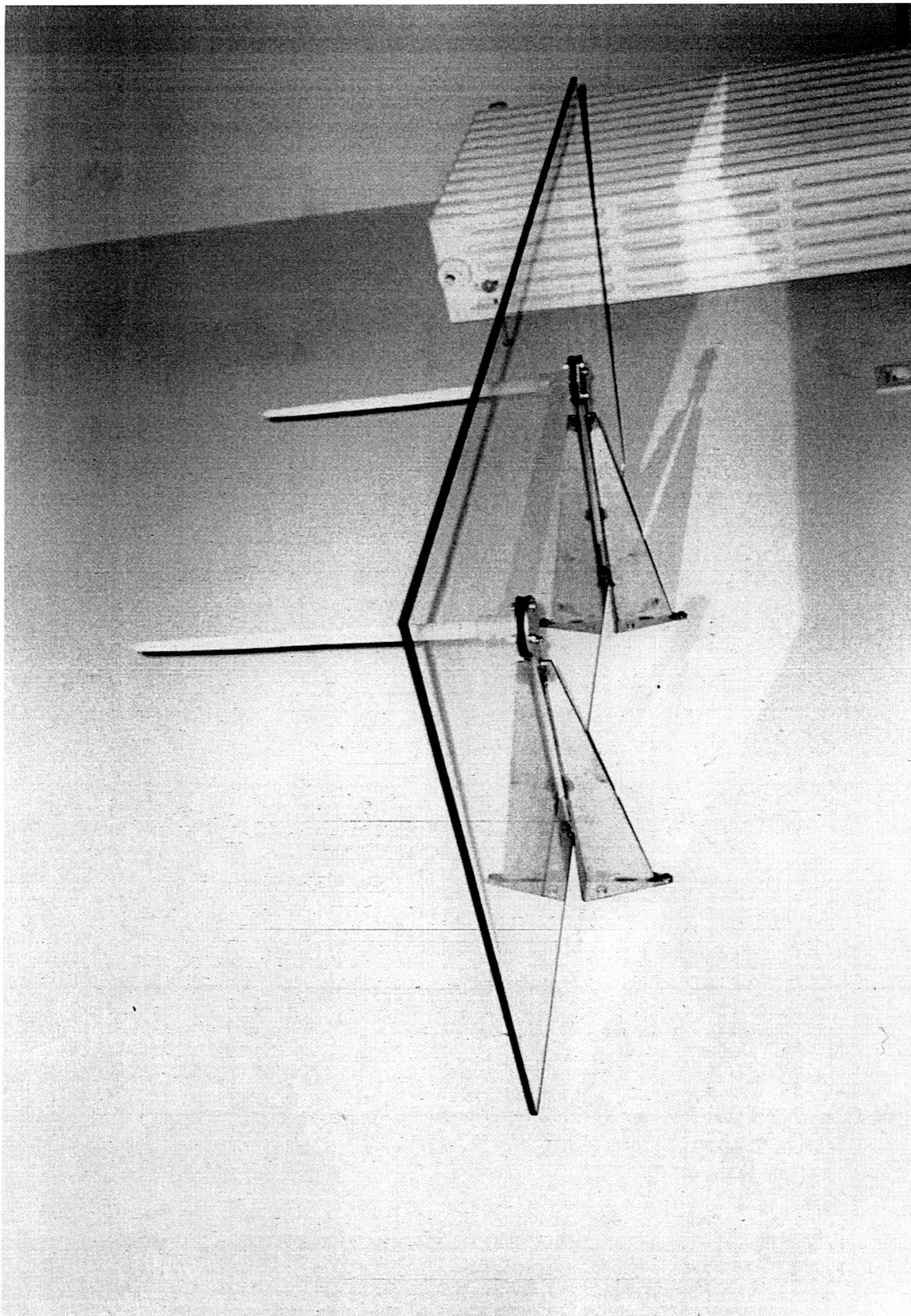

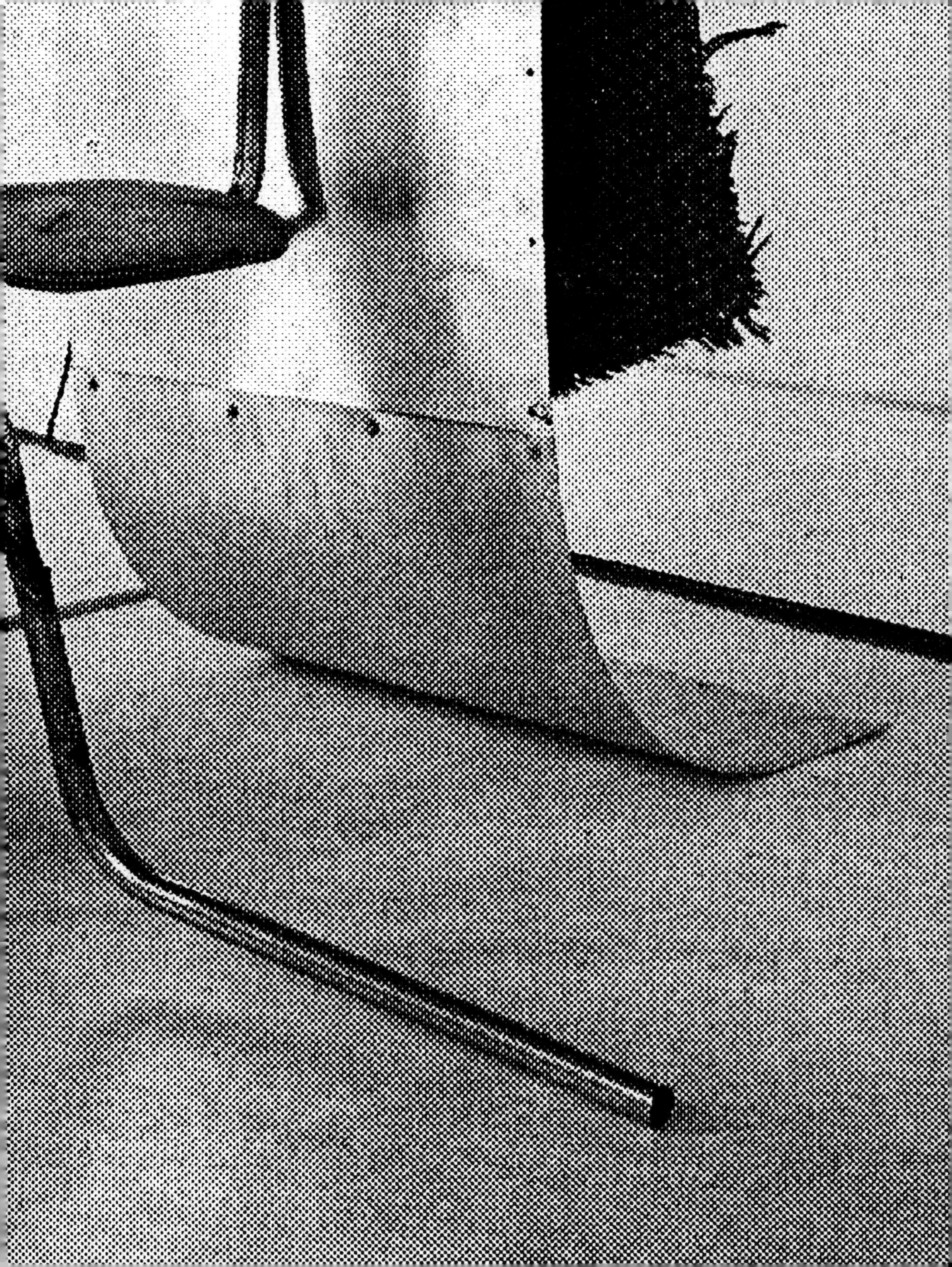

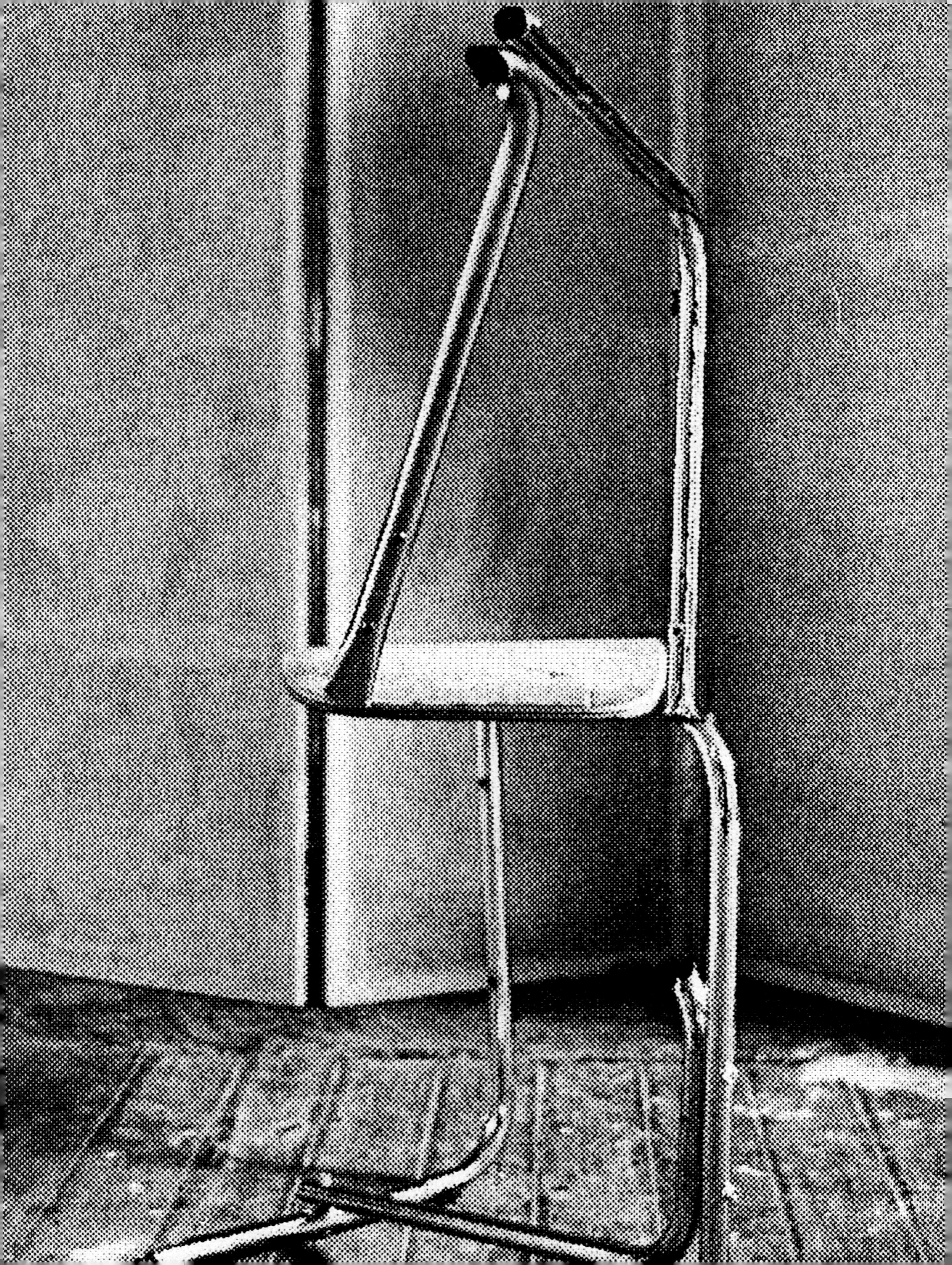

CLOSE
DOOR ALWAY'S
Poort Altijd toe
FerMe LA Porte

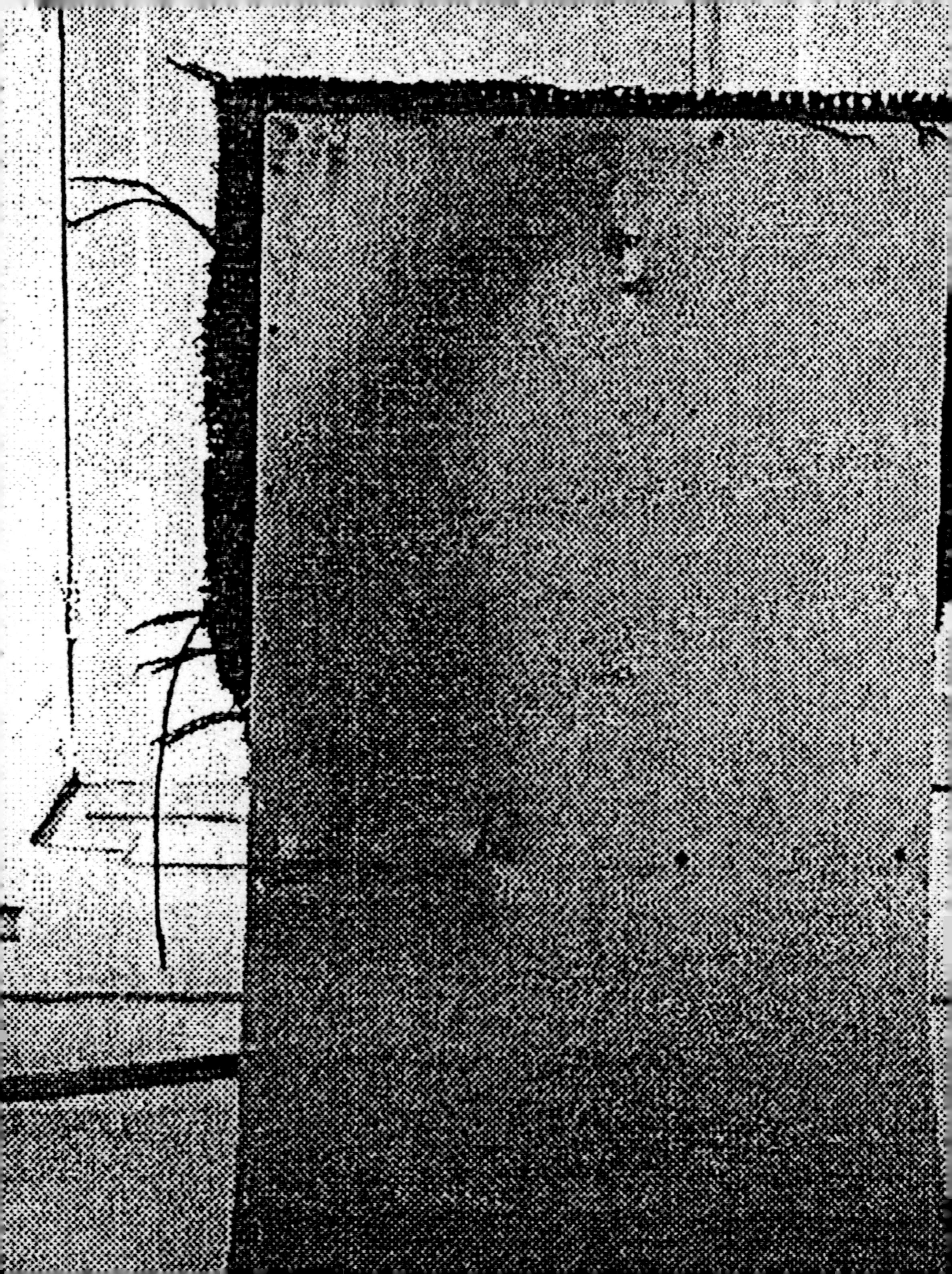

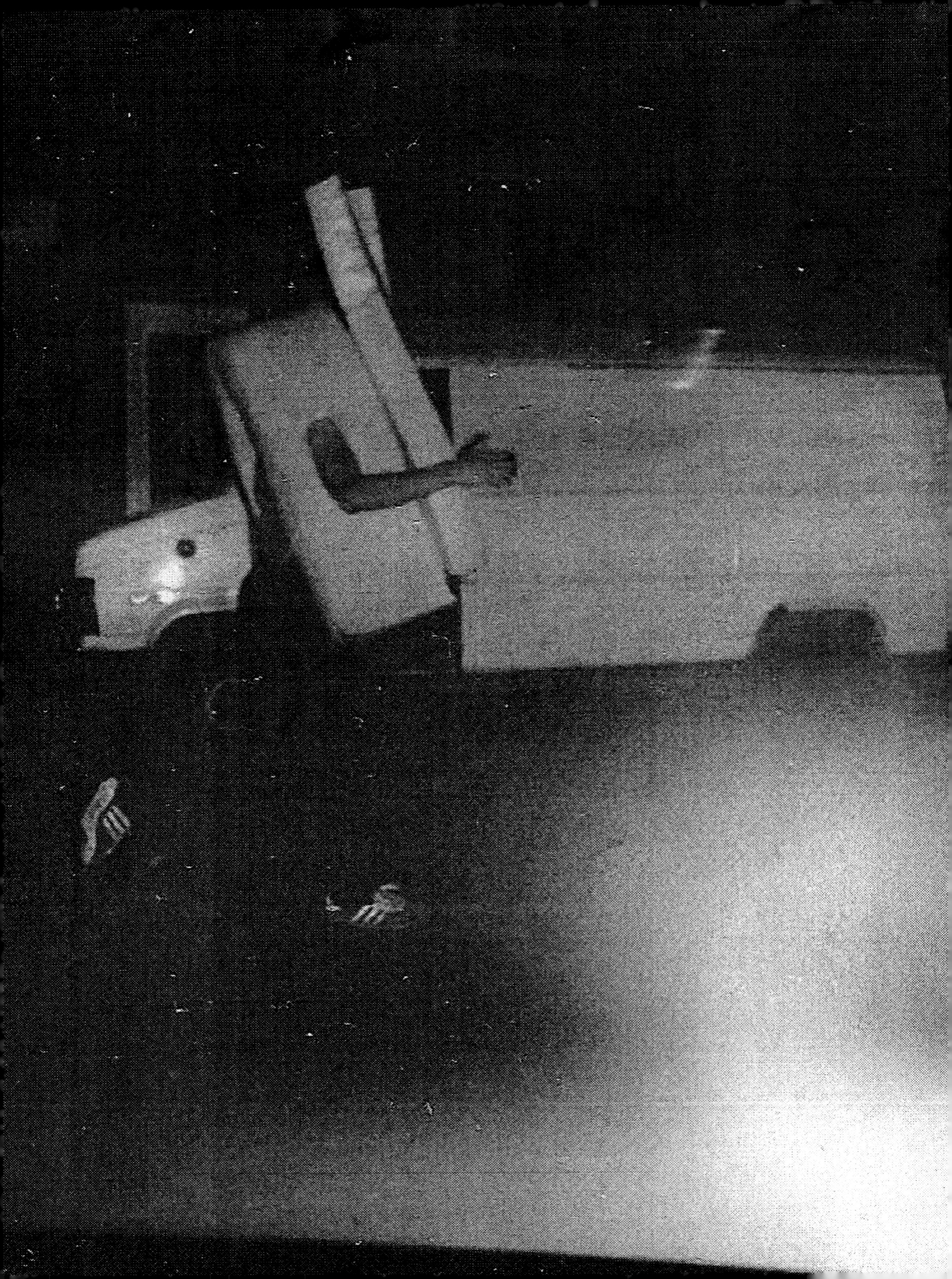

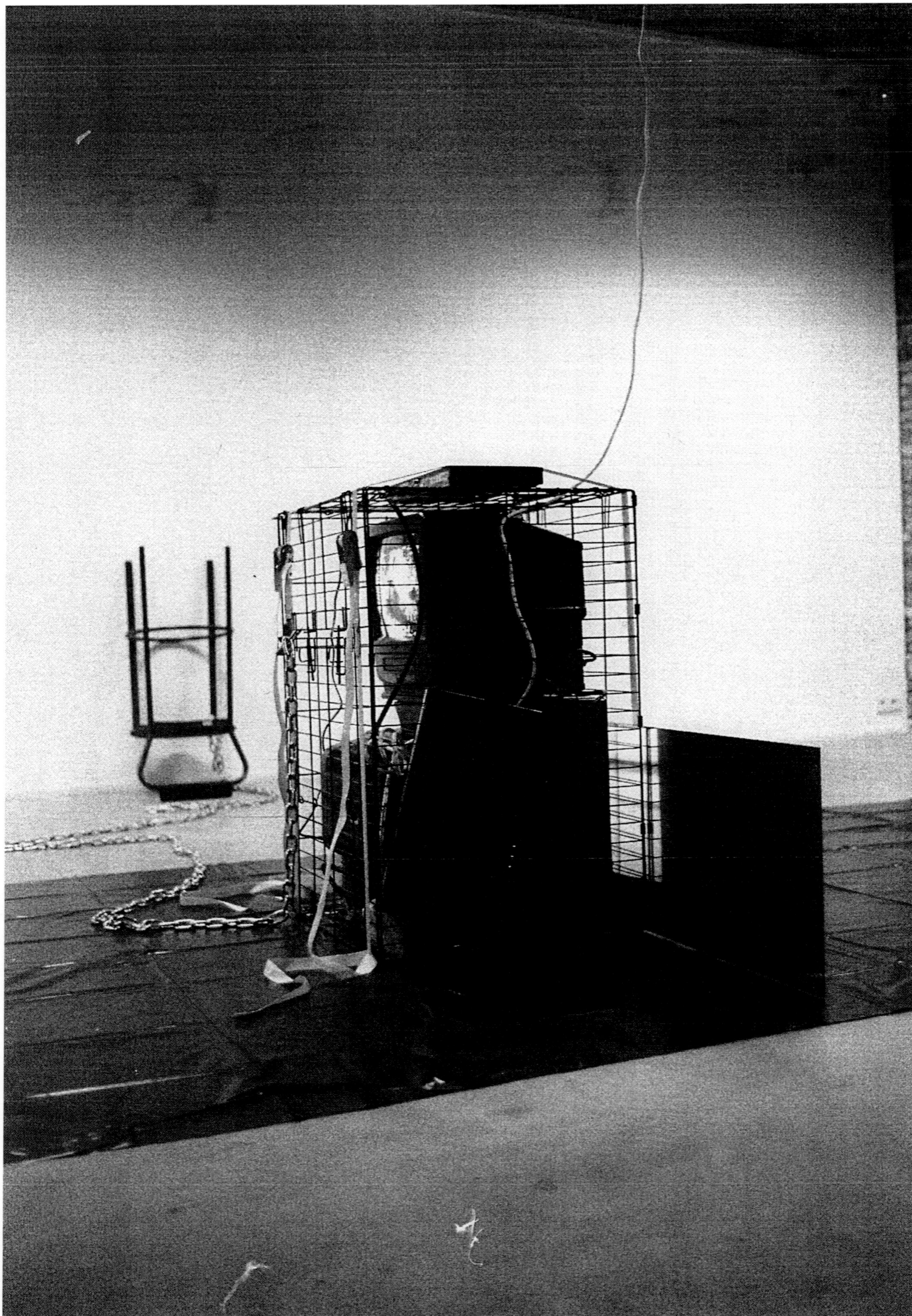

BAYER

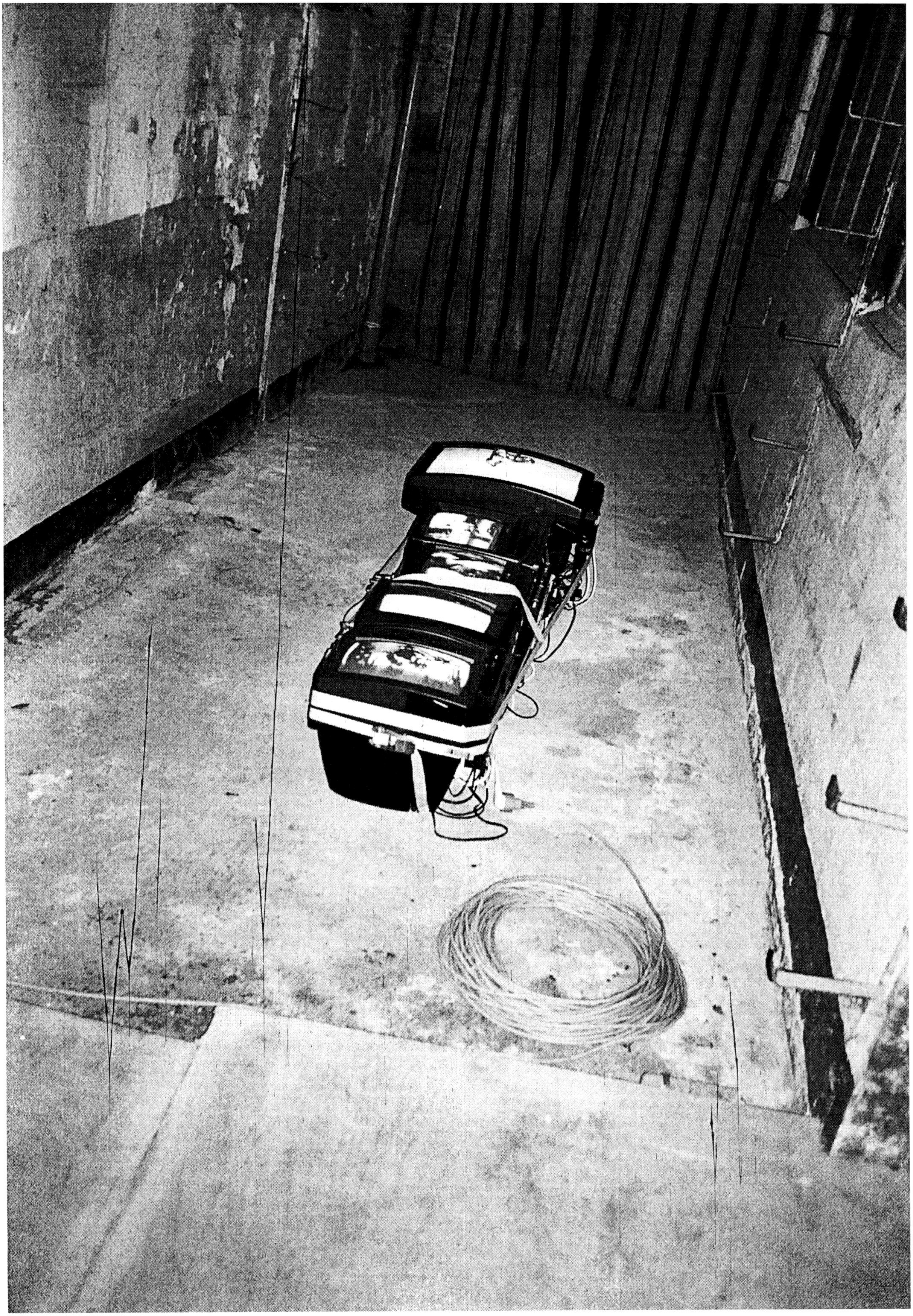

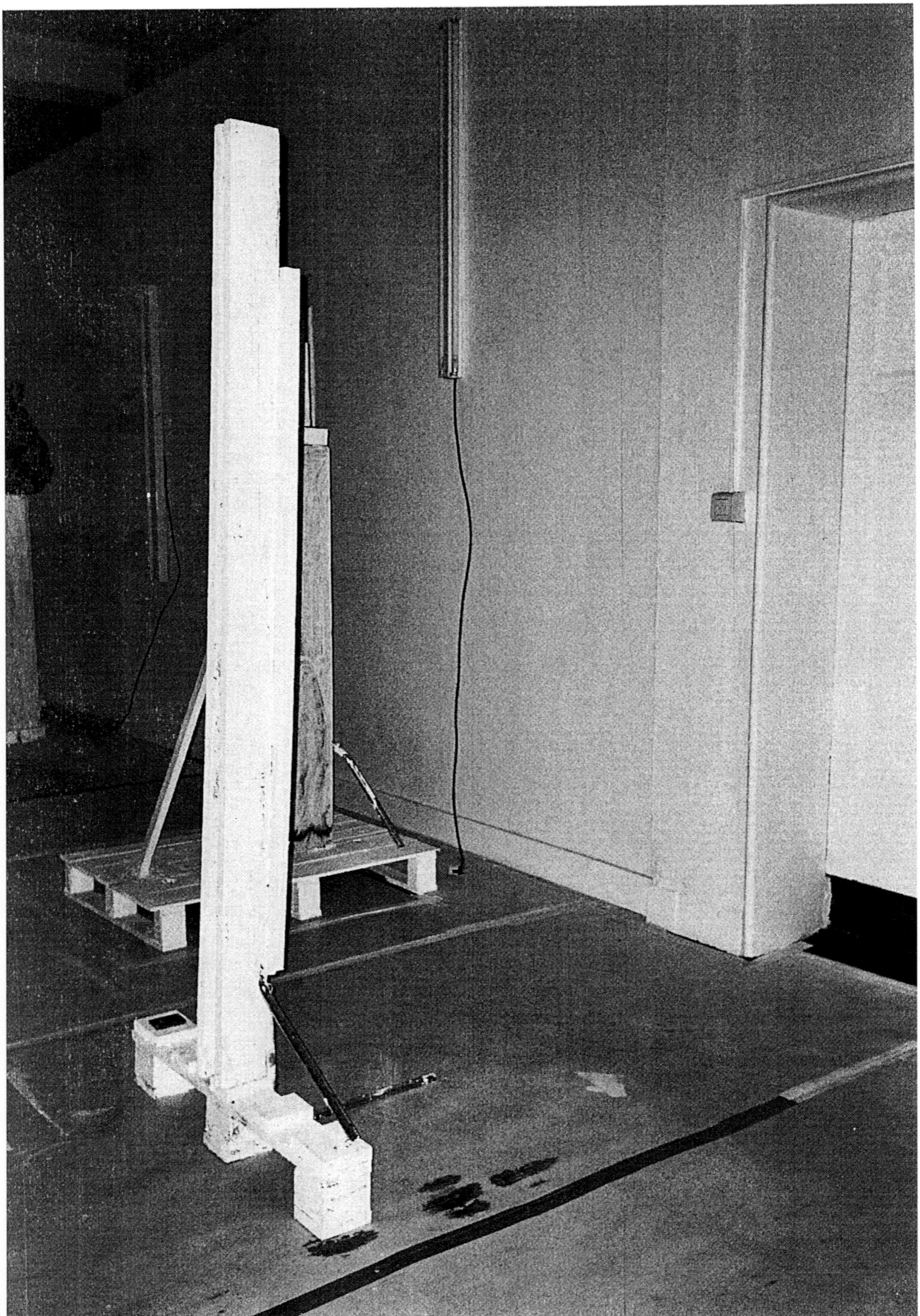

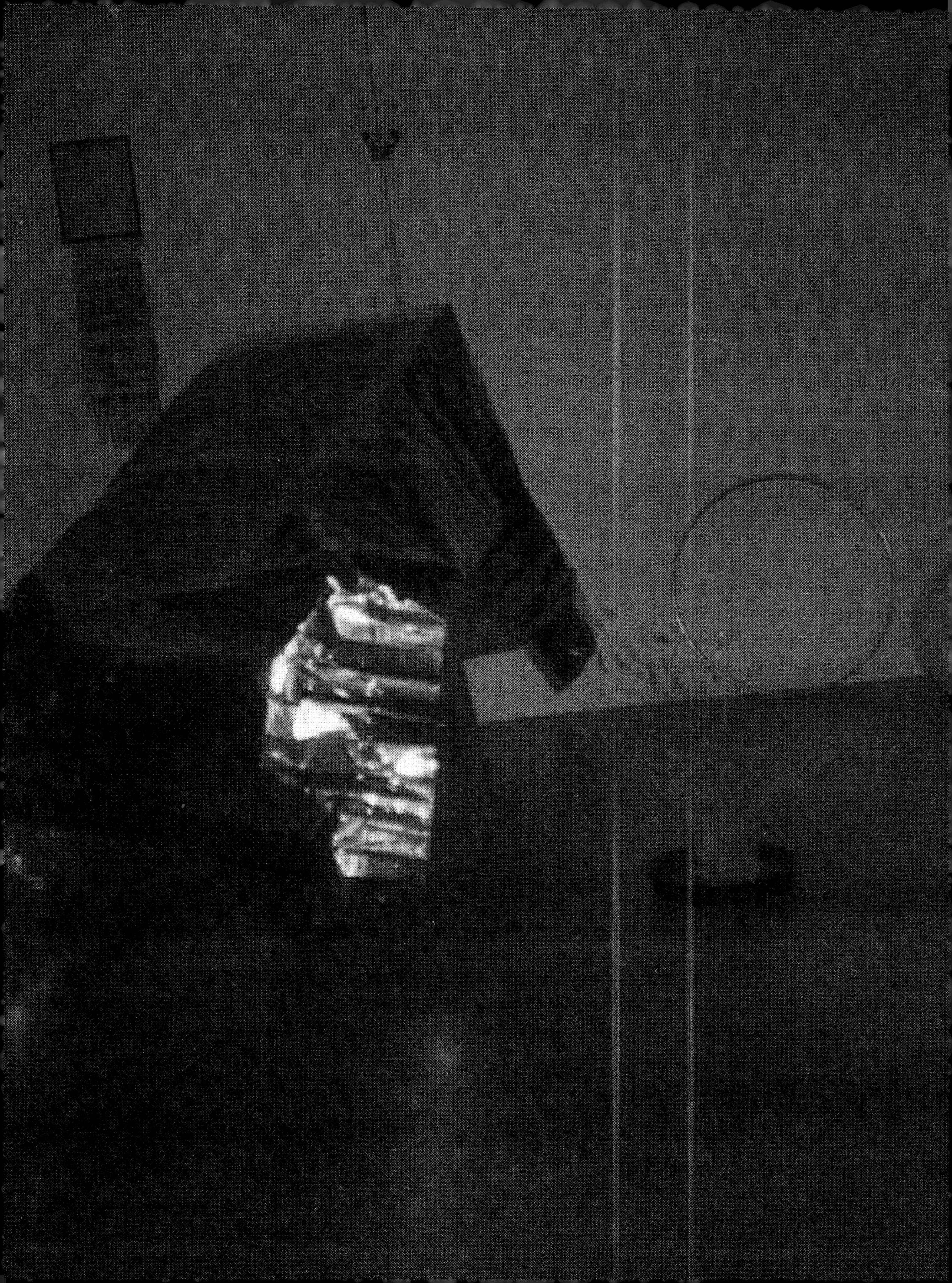

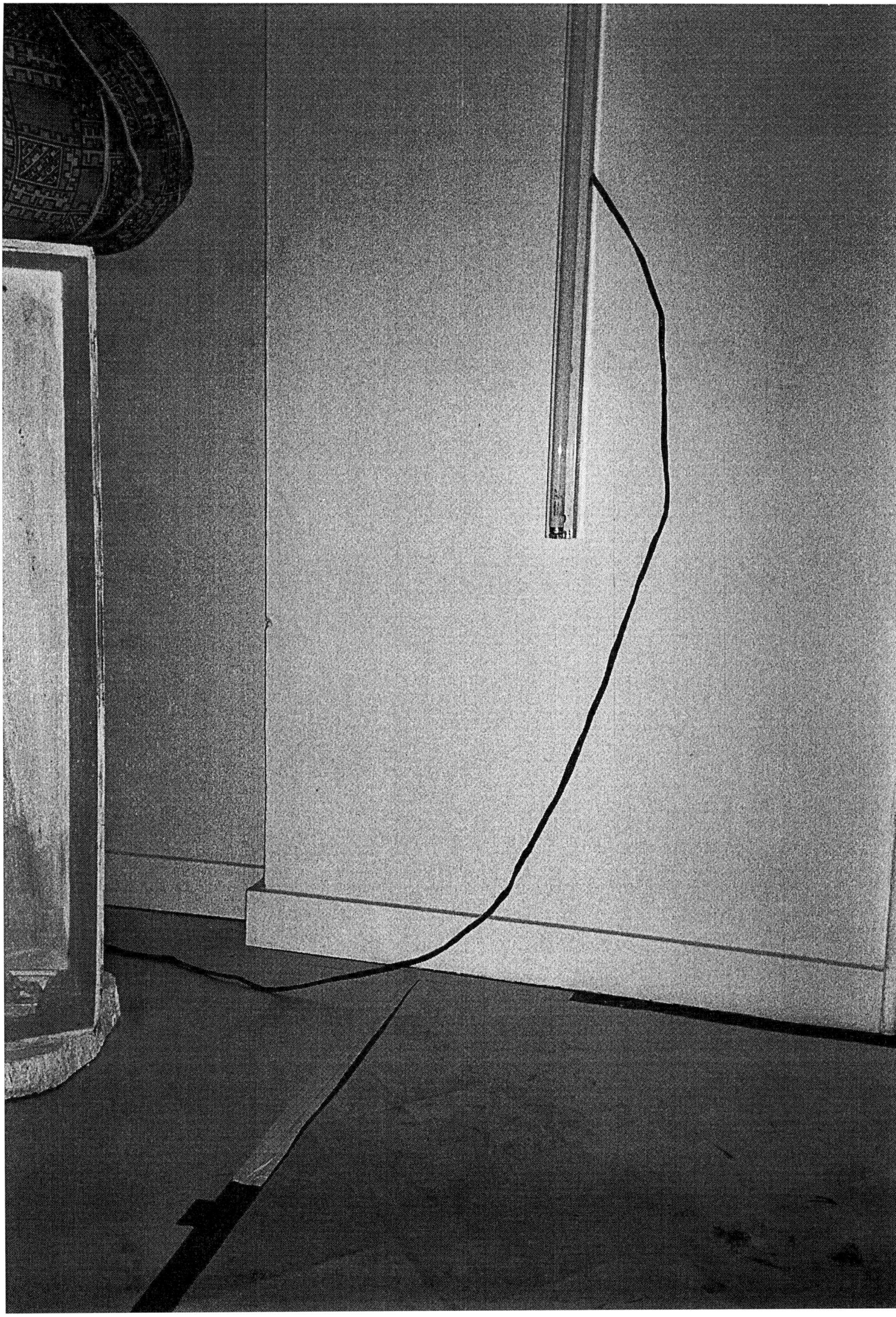

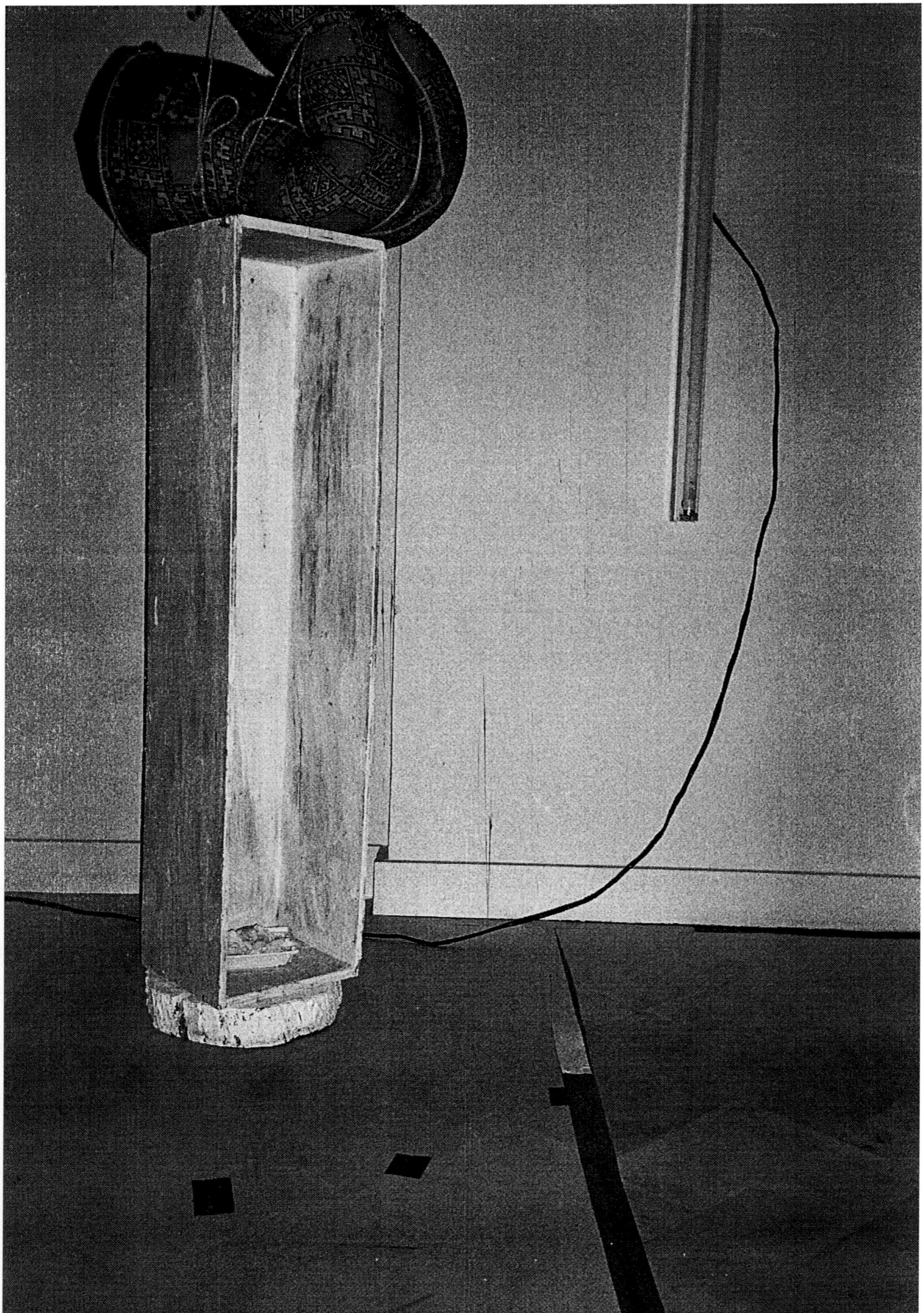

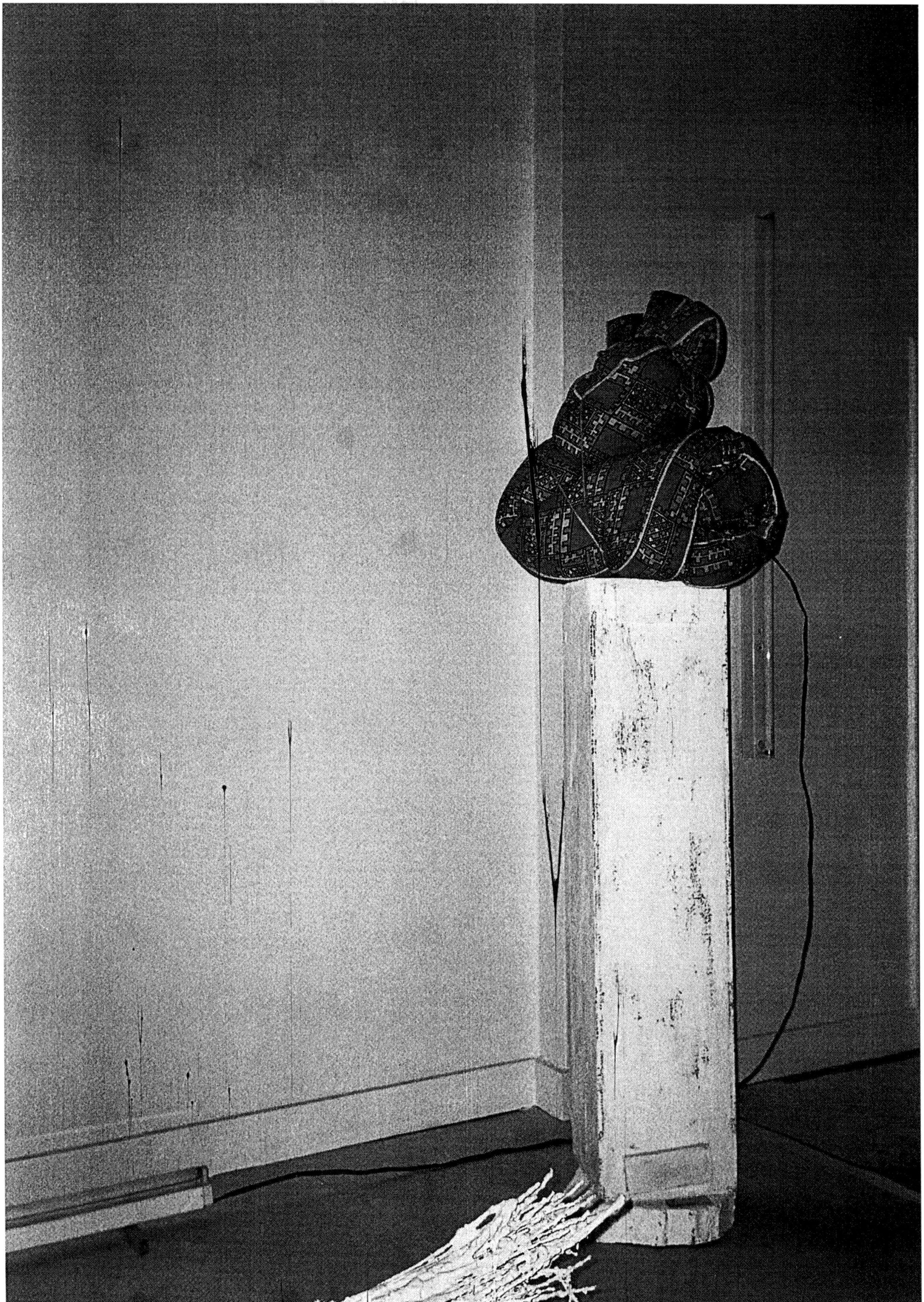

CLOSE
DOOR

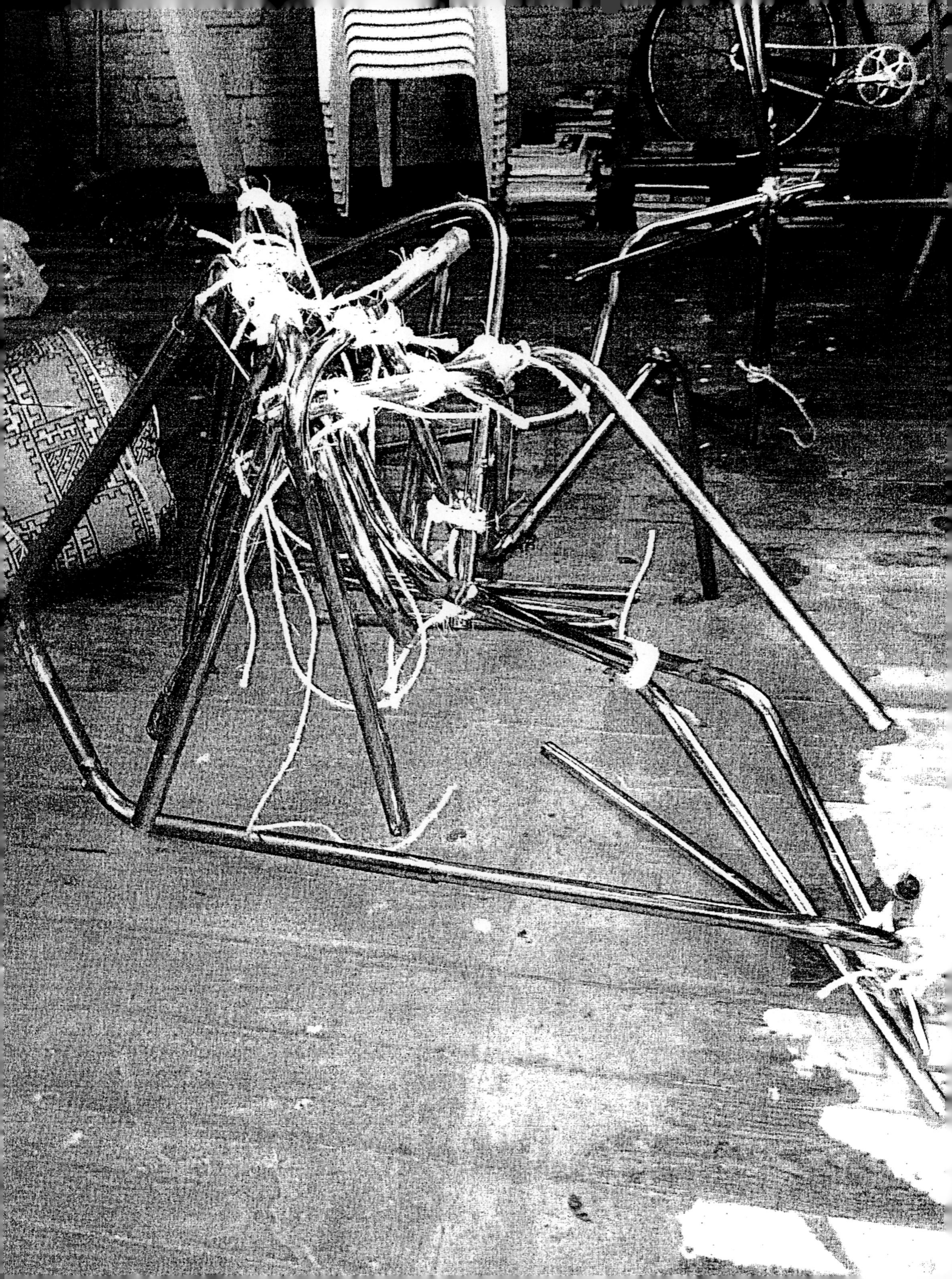

BALNEARIO

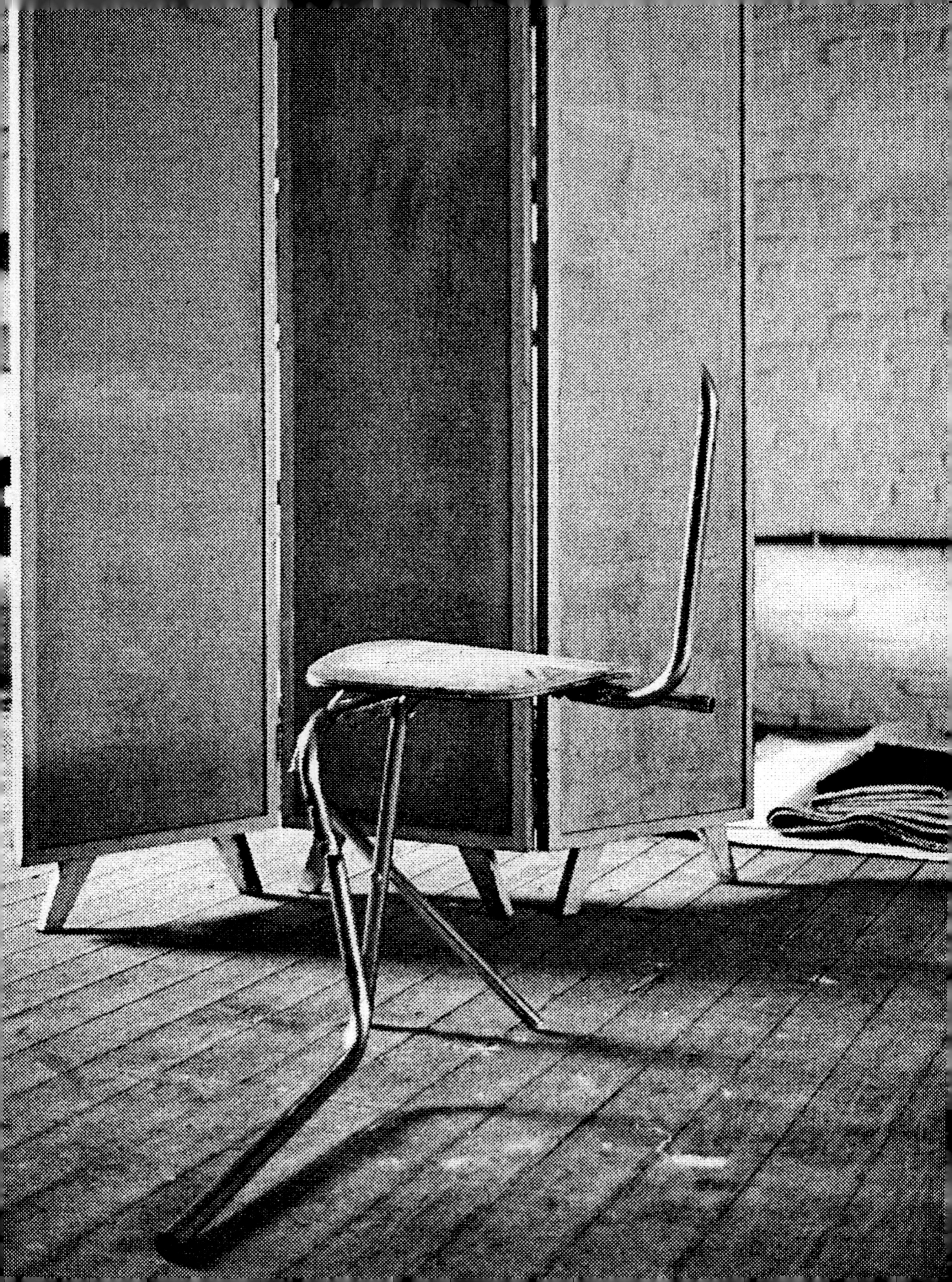

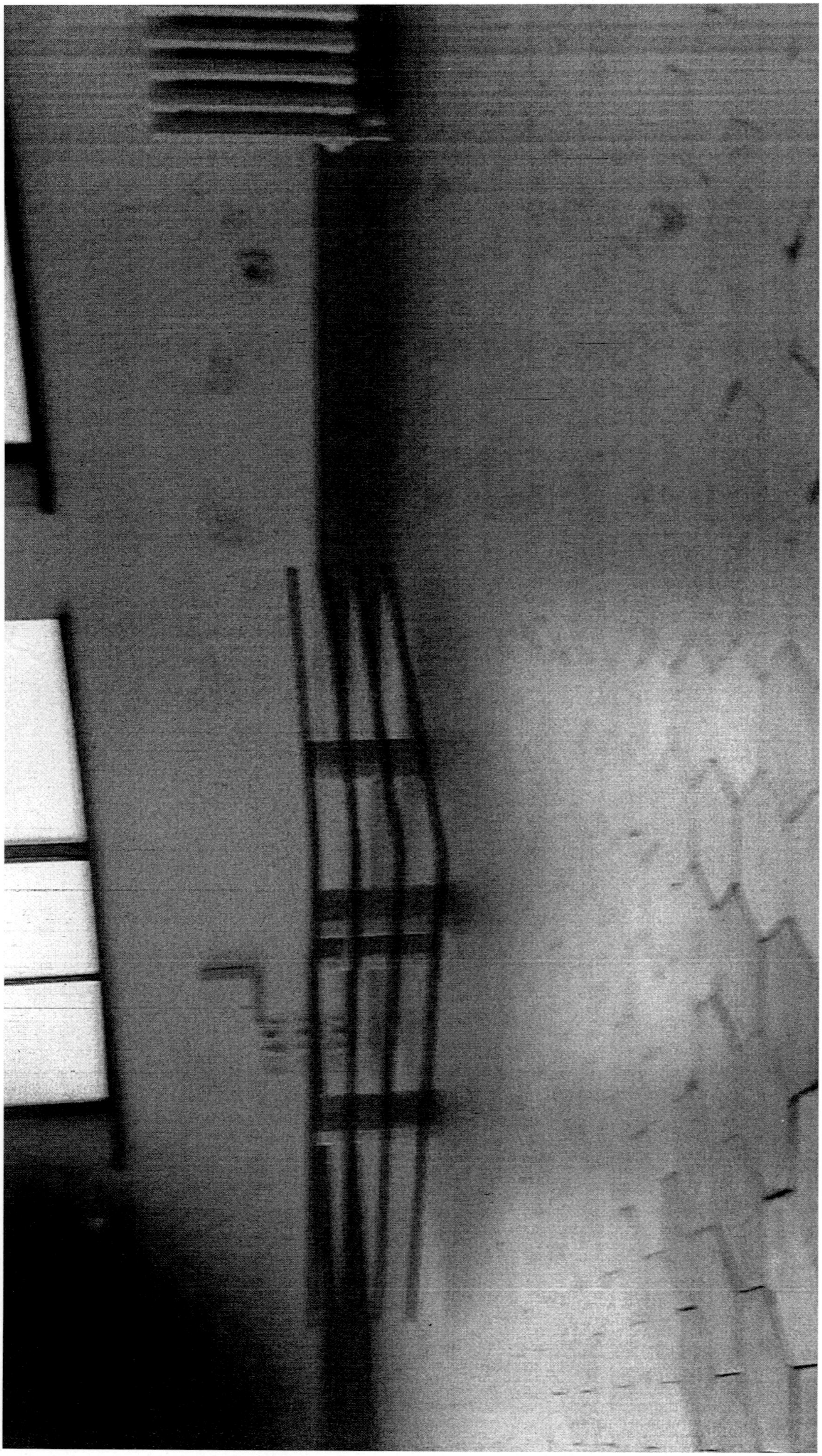

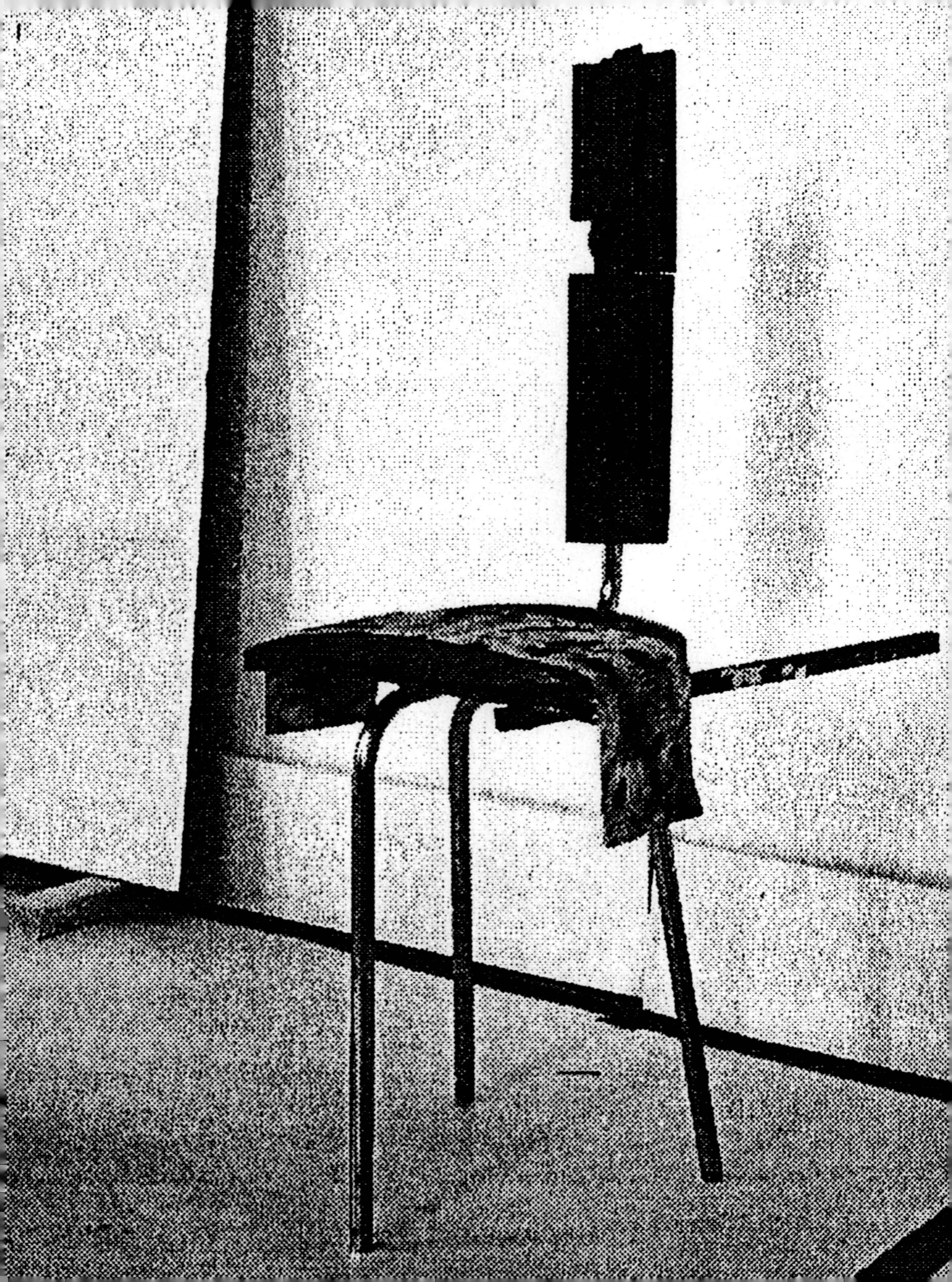

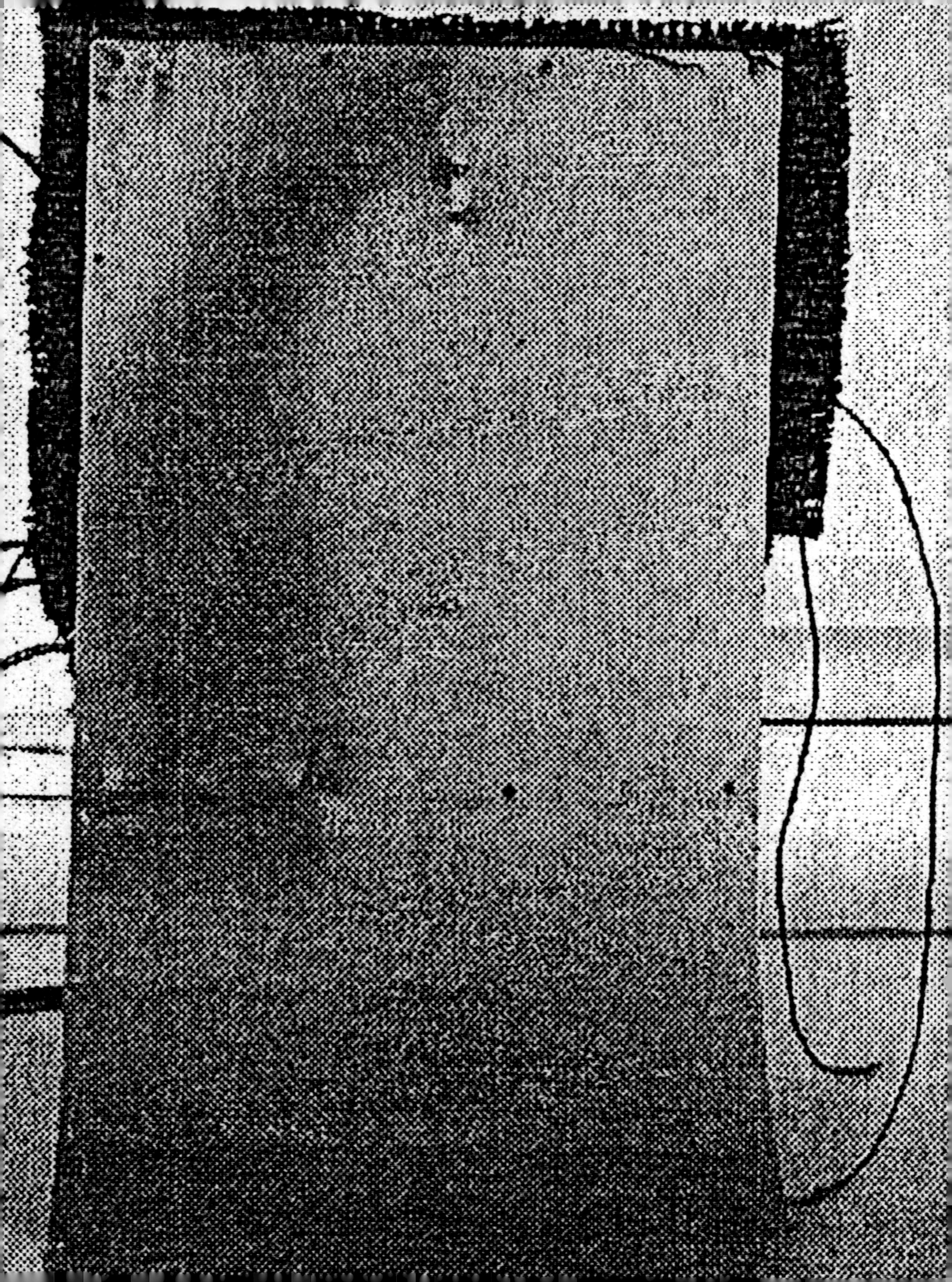

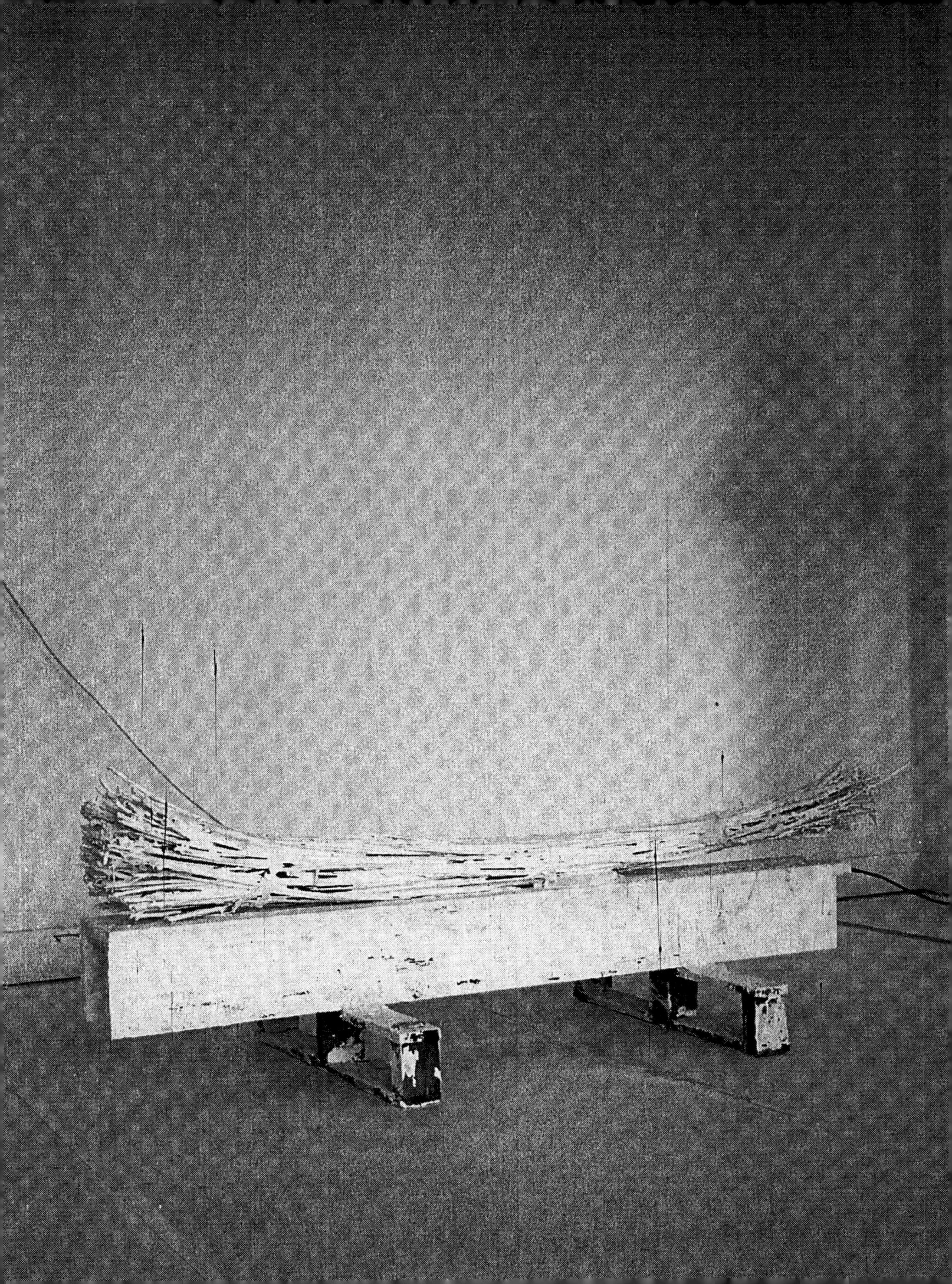

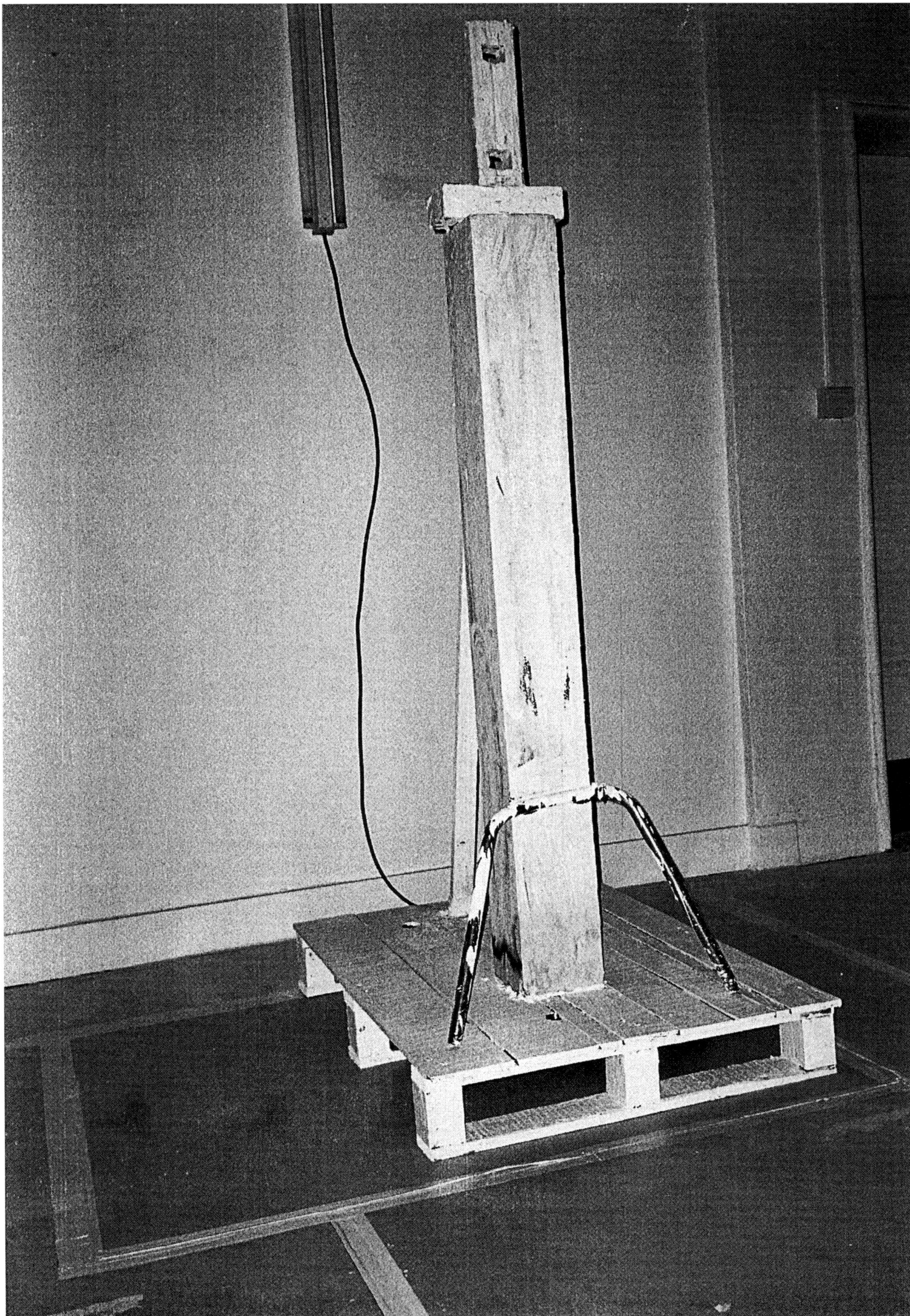

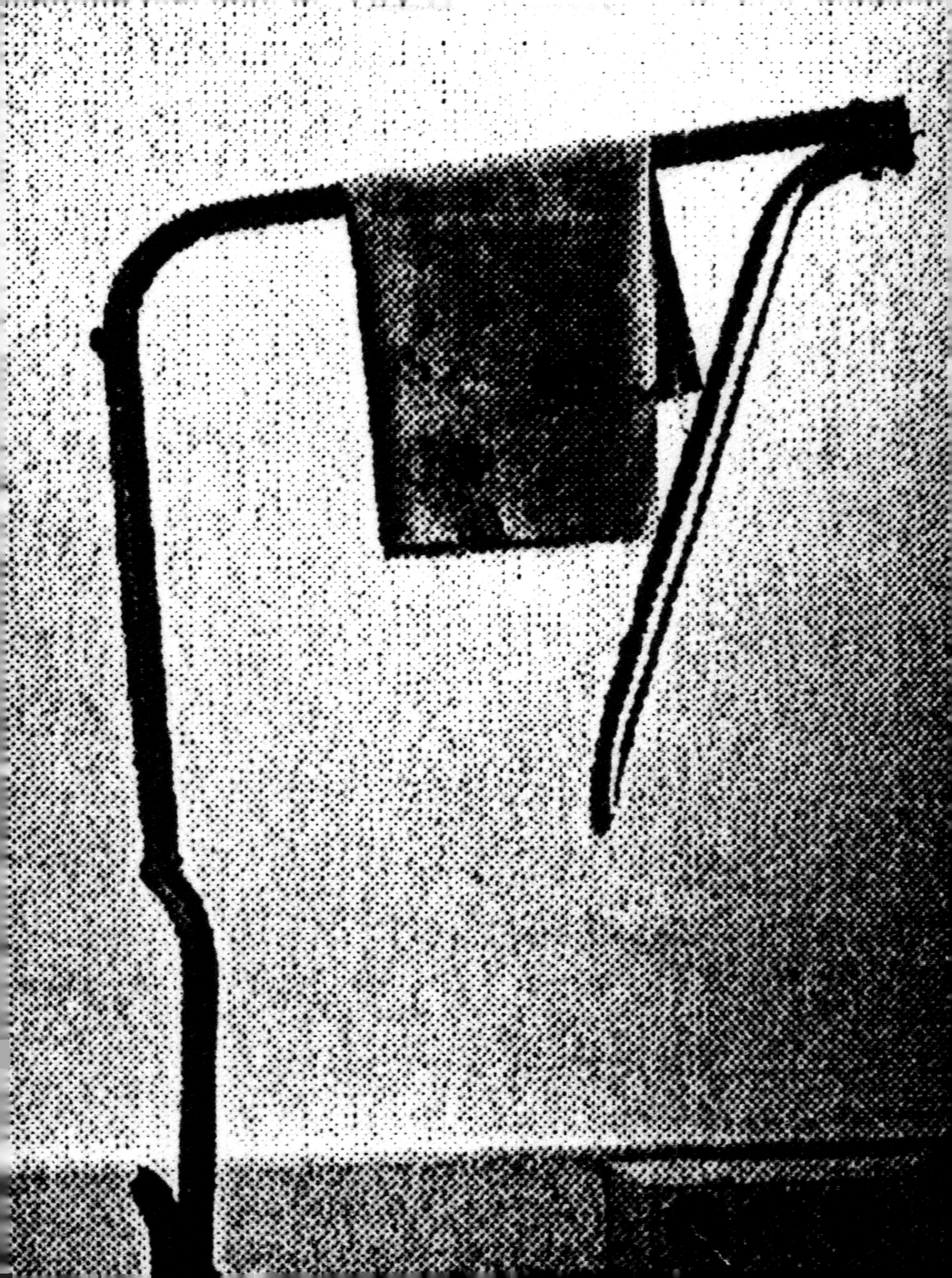

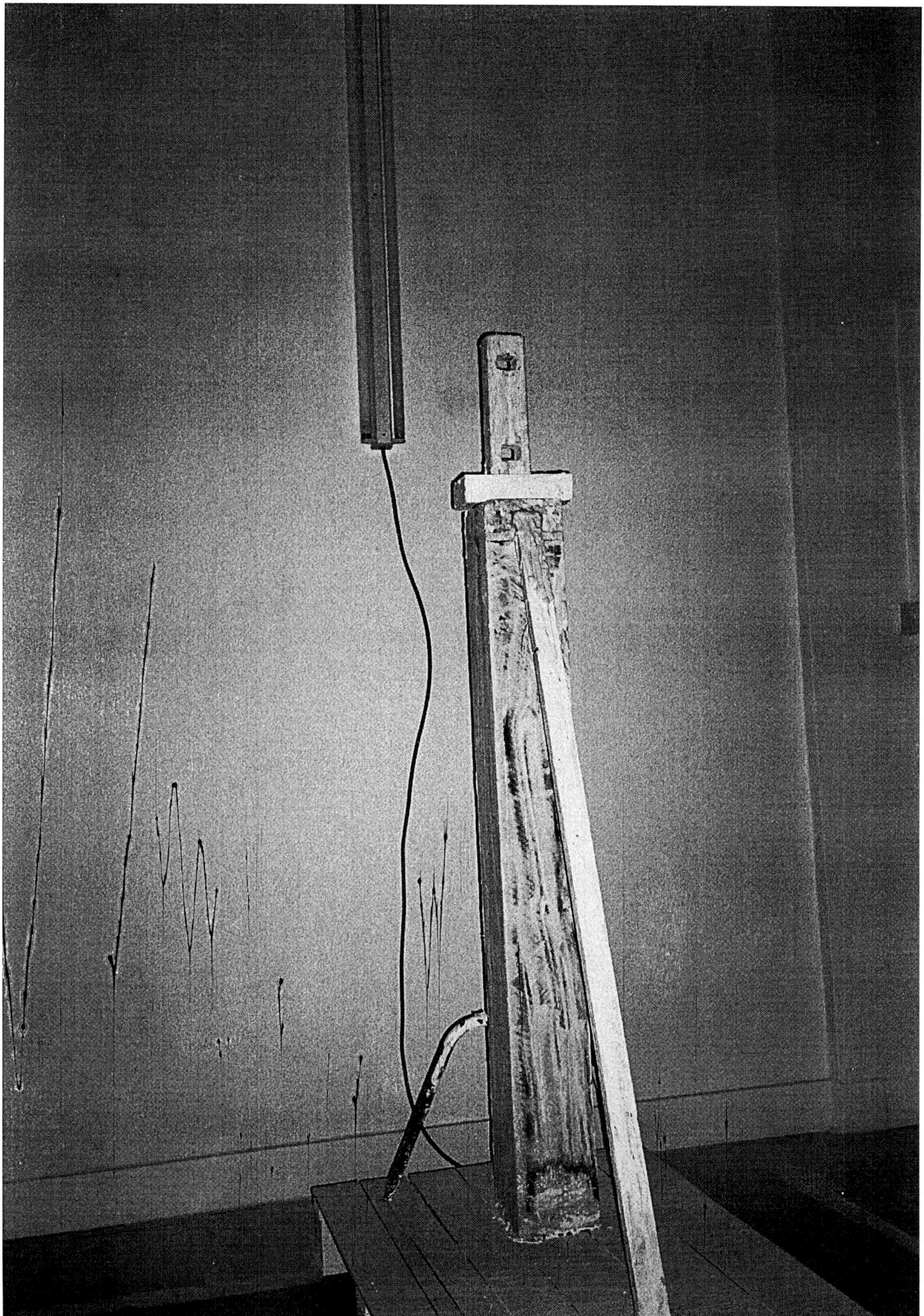

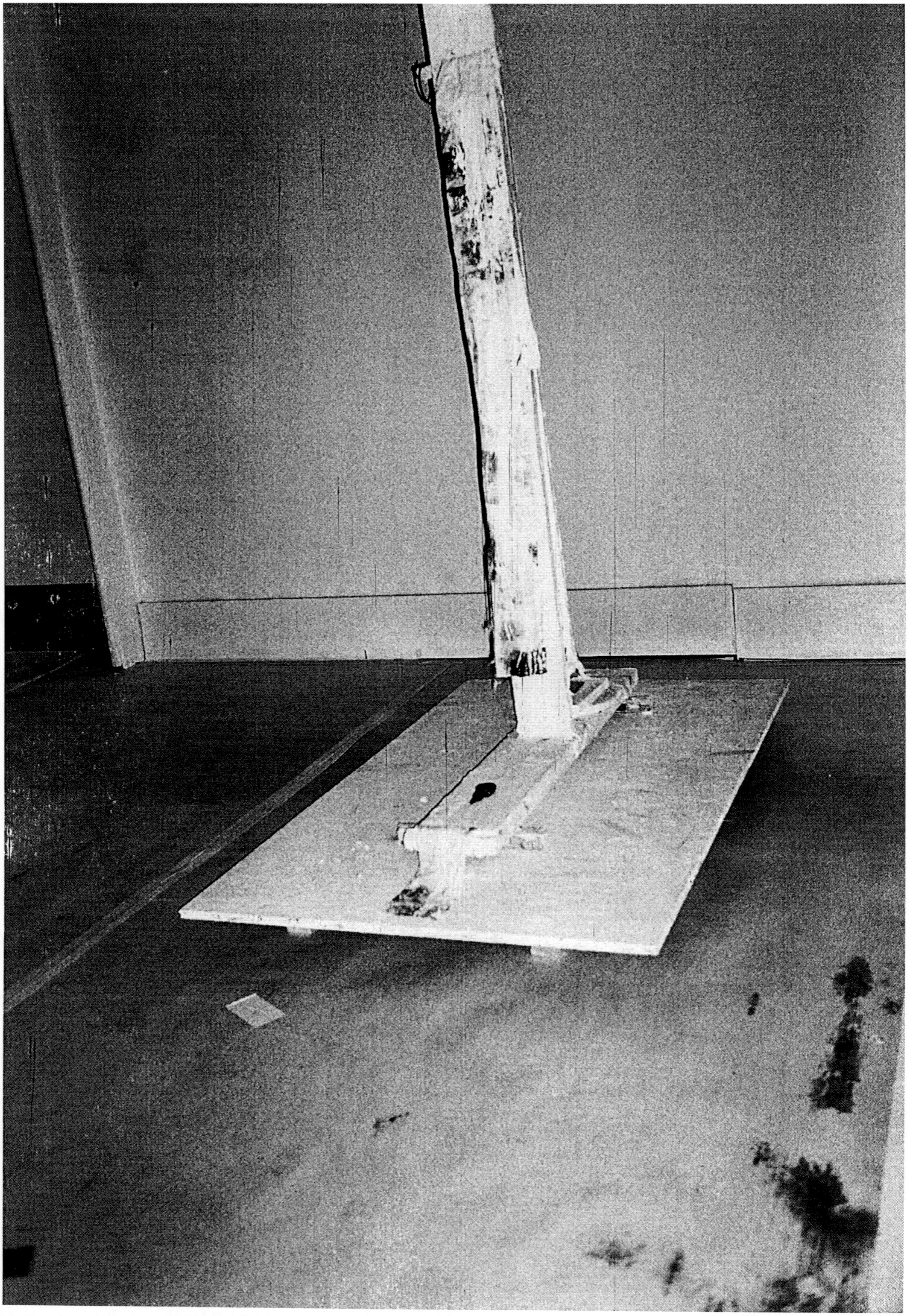

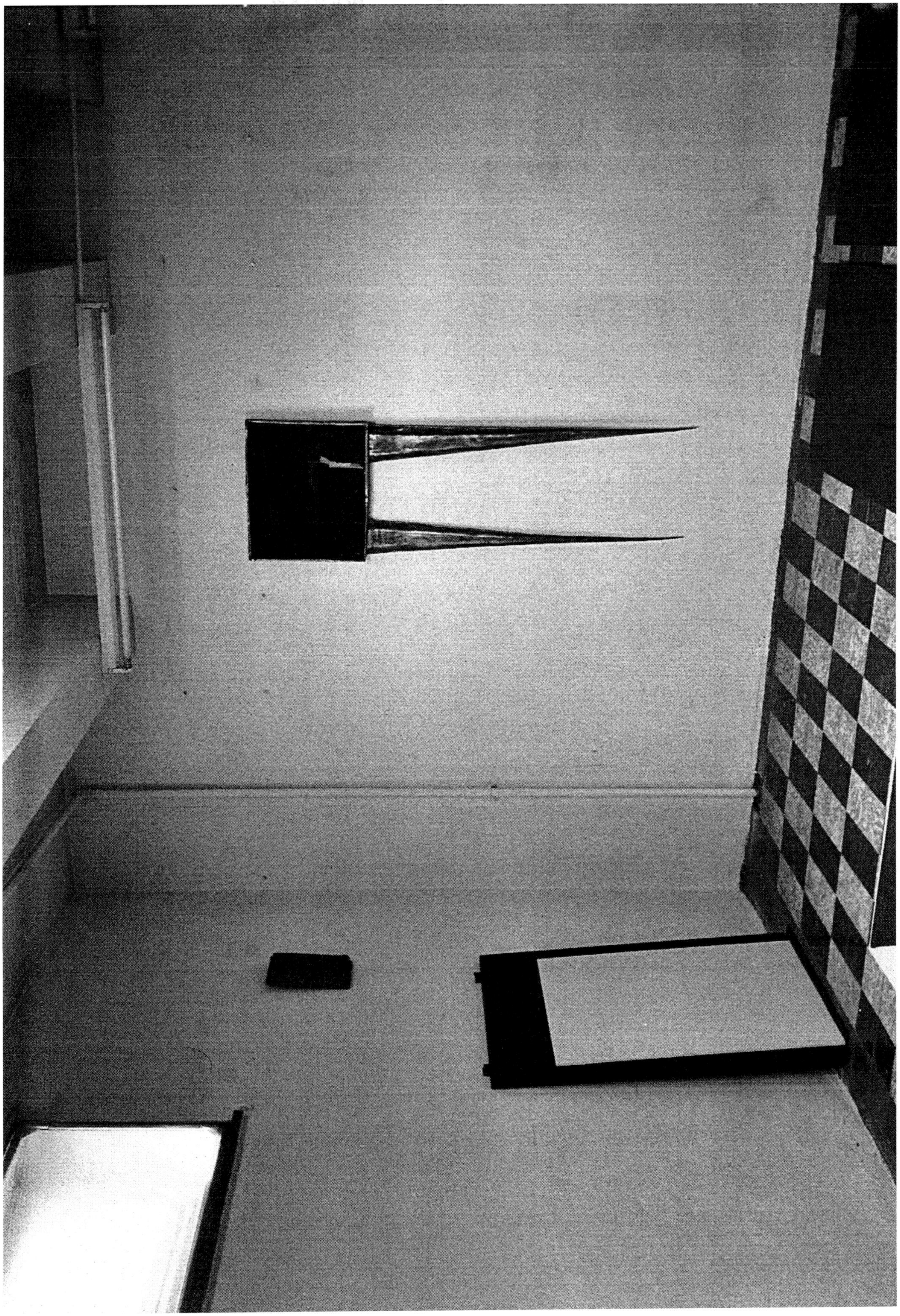

Fix
All

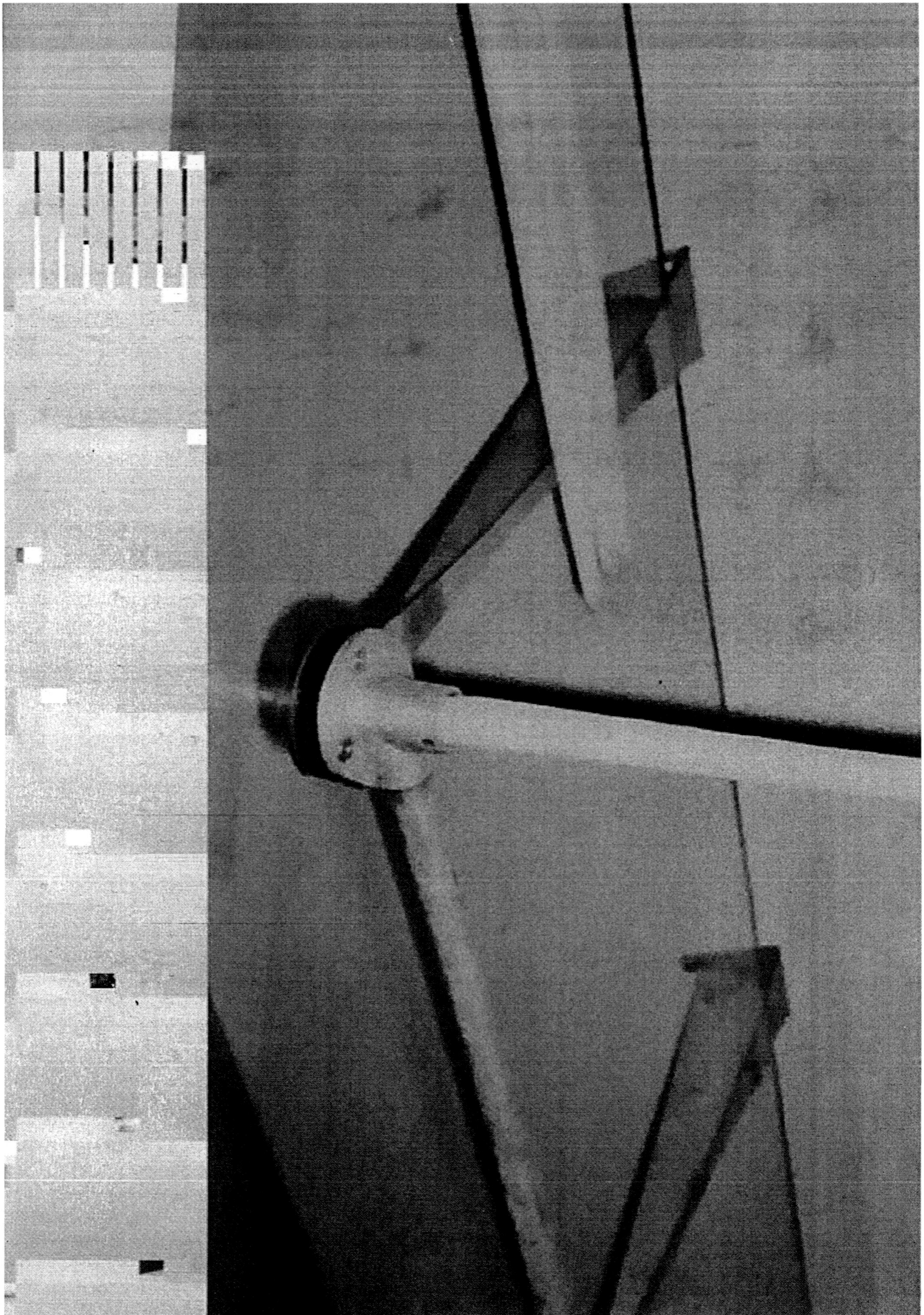

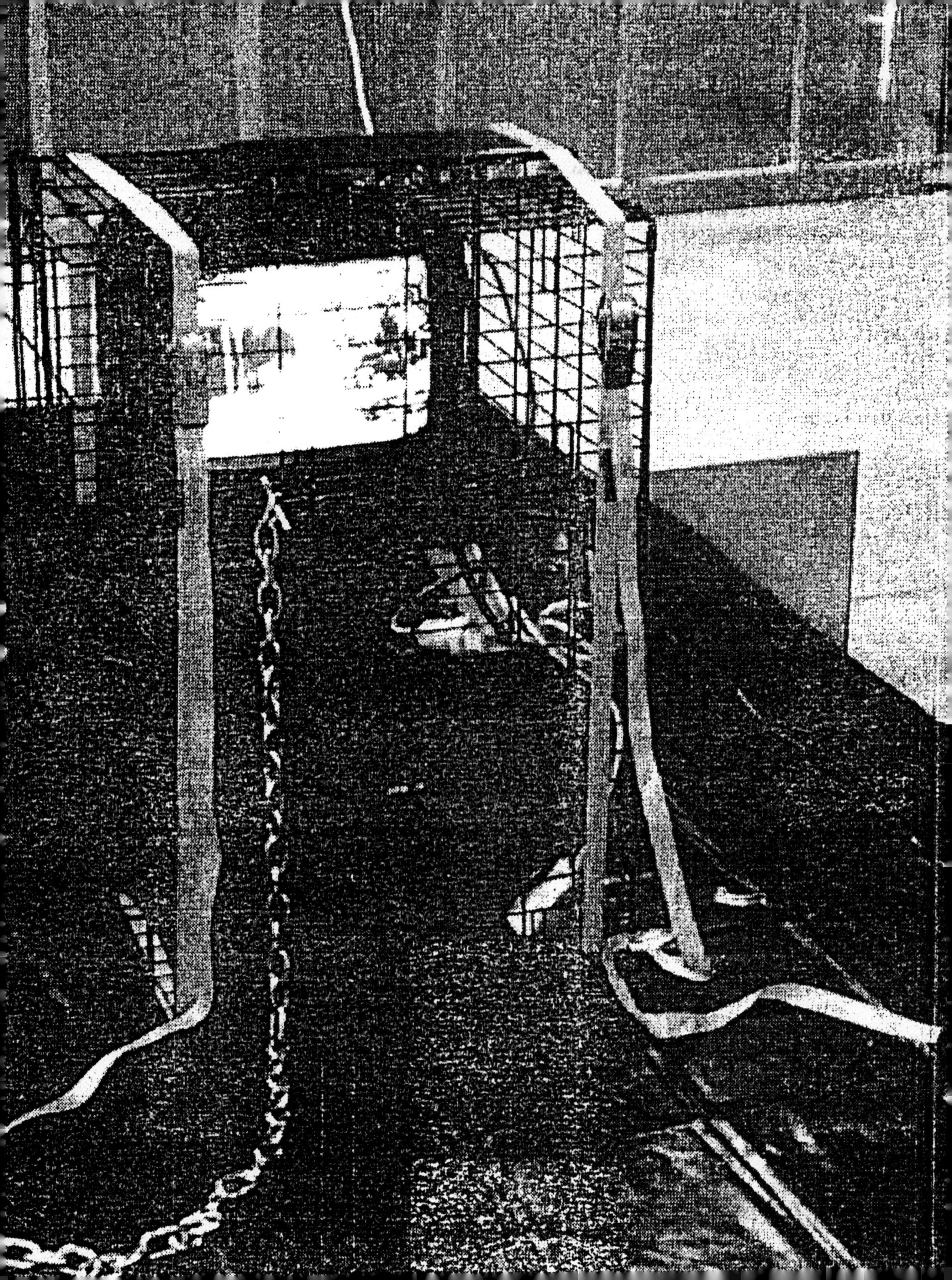

Frais Caprices

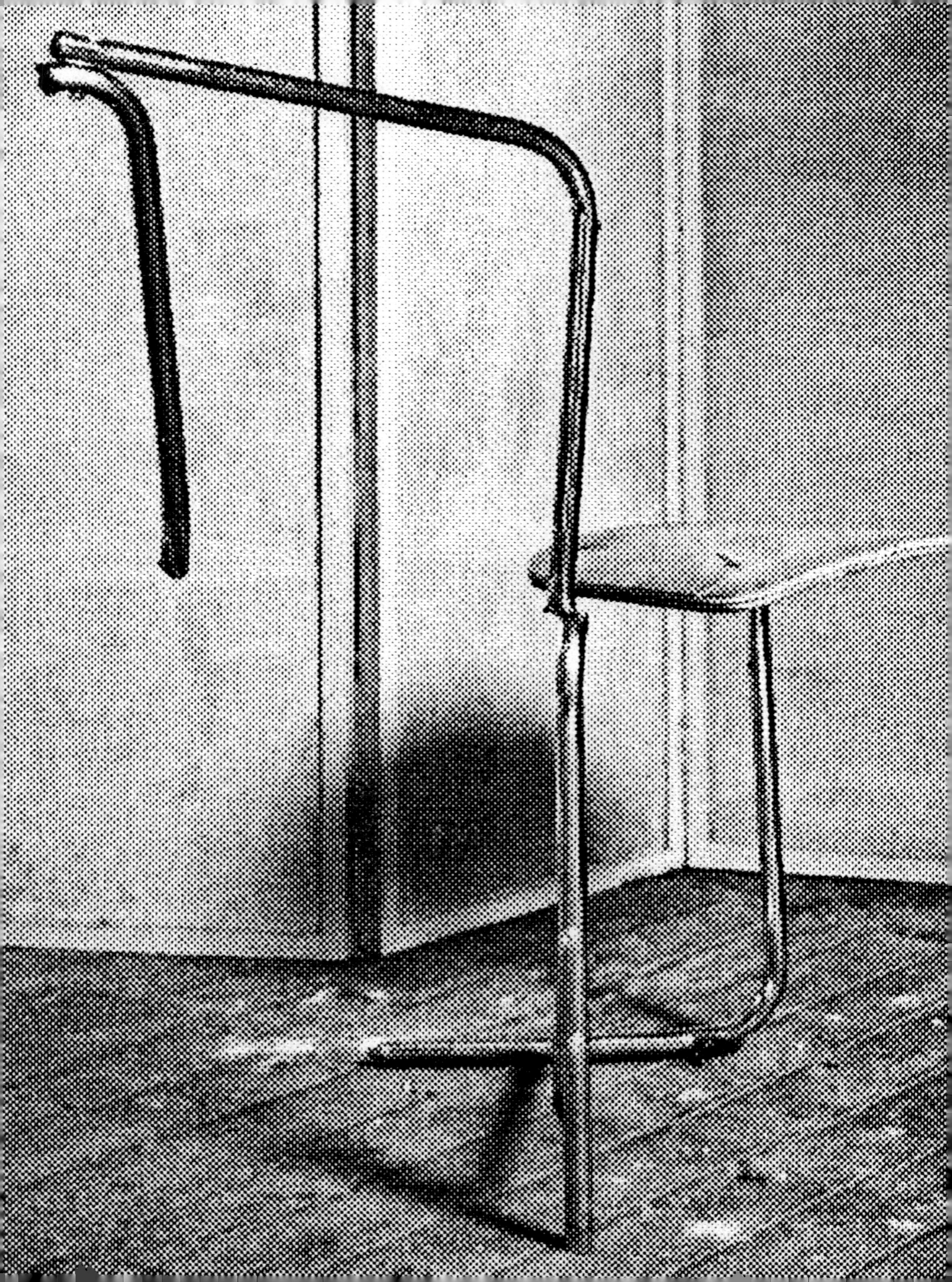

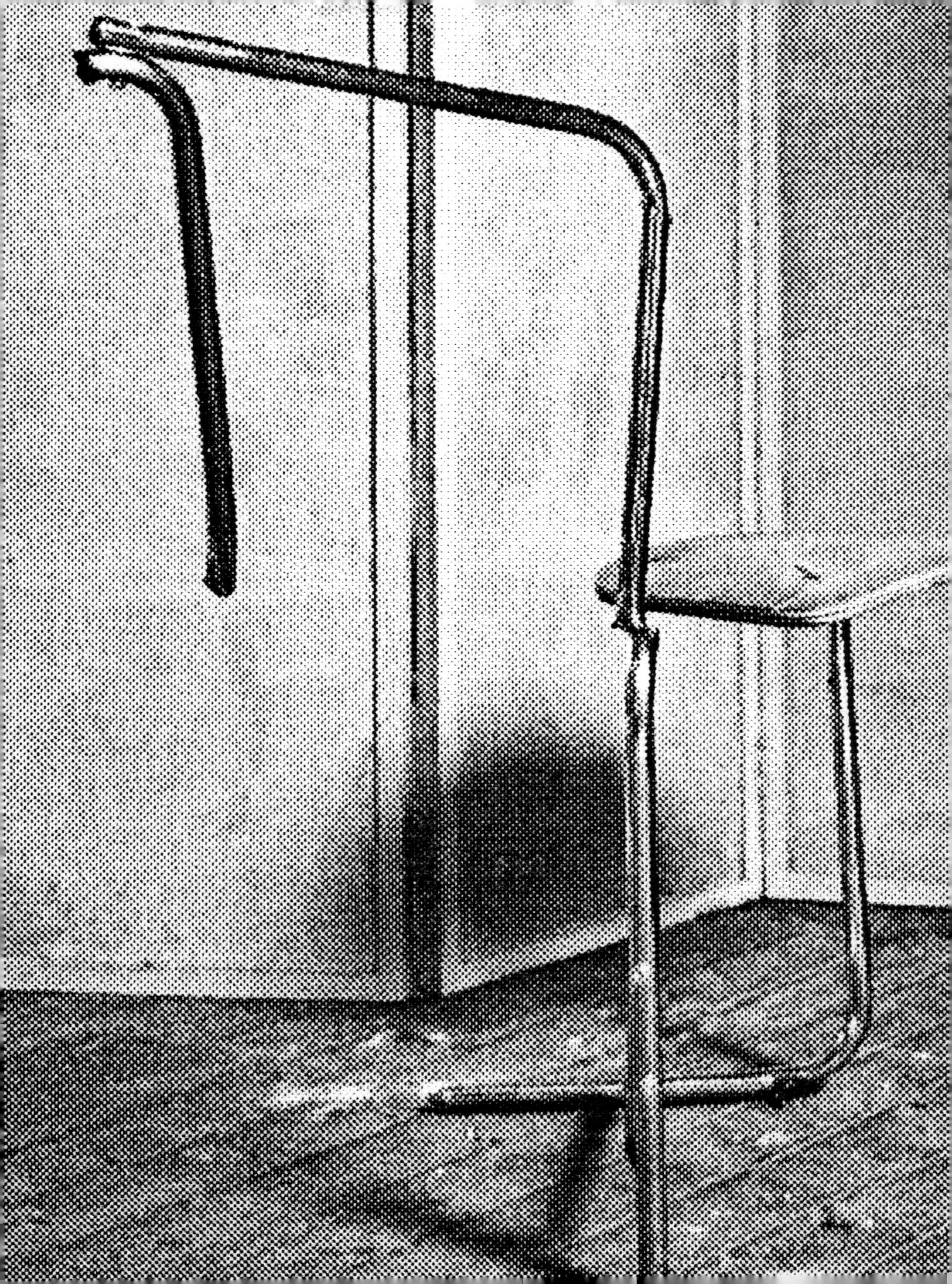